Second

Chances

J. L. Coates

Library and Archives Canada Cataloguing in Publication

J. L. Coates

ISBN-13: 978-0-9880735-0-0

ISBN-10: 0988073501

Printed in USA by Createspace

DEDICATION

To my daughters Christene and Heather,
Two of the bravest strongest
young women I know.
Love you lots.

ACKNOWLEDGEMENTS

Thank you to Clarice Nelson for reading the rough drafts and sharing your ideas. A special thank you to my editor Dianne Tchir, who put aside her personal grief to make this book possible.

I appreciate both of you.

You are not who your past says you are

But

You are who you choose to be today.

Author Unknown

ONE

Faith Benson's hand shook as she picked out the letter from Northrup, Amos and Partners Law office from the pile of mail sitting on the hall table. This was one of the letters she had been waiting for. Next week she would graduate from College as a Legal Assistant, and as a requirement of their Communication and Job Preparation course each student had to send a resume to five law firms. On a whim, she had chosen one of the most prestigious firms in the city of Lancaster located about two hundred miles from her home. Now she held their response in her hands.

Upon finishing high school Faith had chosen to live at home and attend their local community college. Now, she was looking forward to leaving and pursuing her career. A letter of acceptance would mean that finally she could leave this small town and its small town ideas. She wanted more from life than what was available to her here.

"Mom, look it's here, an answer from Northrup and Amos. You open it. My hands are shaking too much." she stuttered, handing the letter to her mother June Benson.

Her mother ripped one corner of the envelope then tore down the side using her finger like a letter opener. Slowly she withdrew the single piece of paper; read the contents then broke into a big smile exclaiming "You did it! They're offering you a job starting on the eleventh of next month. If you accept their offer you have to call a lady named Elizabeth Heatley. She will go over the details with you."

Snatching the letter from her mother's hand Faith slowly read the letter for herself. "Can you believe this? I almost didn't apply. Of course I accept. This is a dream come true, my one chance to move away from here."

"This doesn't give us much time. You only have fourteen days to finish your finals, graduate, and for us to find you a place to live. Go phone this lady right now and tell her you are going to take the job." insisted her mother. She understood Faith's reasons for wanting to move away from home and didn't blame her. At twenty-one it was hard for her to still have to follow her father's strict rules and not be able to do what her friends were doing.

Faith was hugging her mother when they heard the front door open then slam shut. Both of them had forgotten how poorly Faith's father, Clive Benson, would react to this news. He would not be happy. As their only child Faith knew he wanted her close by, staying home, finding a nice boy and raising a family but her plans were very different.

When she had initially made plans to go away to college, she and her dad had fought bitterly. She wanted to get away from his heavy drinking and drunken rants. He was violently opposed to every idea she had.

In the end, she based her decision to remain at home upon cost. Her parents couldn't afford to send her away to school. Faith gave into his demands deciding that life would be easier for her and her mother if she stayed where she was.

The intensive course meant she spent most her time at home studying and had little, if any, active social life. When she did go out, her father's rules were very strict; home by eleven. She decided to go along with his demands until she graduated, then she would leave and live on her own terms.

"Hey girls, what's up?" he said slurring his words. "What are you so happy about?"

Faith looked over at her mother then blurted out "I got a job with one of the top law firms in Lancaster and start in two weeks."

Both she and her mother should have realized this was not the right time to break the news to him. His eyes were red and bleary. It was plain to see he had started drinking early today.

"You ain't going" he said. "You ain't moving to no city by yourself."

"Dad?"

"I said you ain't going and that's final."

Faith looked at him long and hard. Tears flooded her eyes as she turned and walked out of the kitchen. When he had been drinking there was no use arguing with him. Maybe tomorrow, if he was sober, they could talk.

"Where you going girl? I'm talking to you."

"Leave her alone Clive. You have said more than enough already." her mother admonished her husband. "Faith, didn't you tell me that you have to study for one more test tomorrow?"

"You are always siding with that girl against me. One of these days you'll be sorry you did that." he muttered drunkenly. "Get me a drink. Can't a man have any peace and quiet when he comes home from work?"

Faith eagerly went to her bedroom. Sitting down at her desk she opened her notes but was too excited to study. "Finally I have my chance. I can't wait get away from him and his drunken outbursts." She left her bedroom door slightly open because she wanted to hear the discussion between her parents.

"Clive, you have to let the girl go," she heard her mother say. "There is nothing here for her."

"My sister Ethel moved to the city filled with big hopes and dreams. You saw what happened to her, ended up whoring around, six kids with six different fathers. Know what she is now? She's a bag lady living on the streets. Is that what you want for Faith?"

"Clive. Stop. You know our Faith isn't like that. She has a good head on her shoulders and will have a very good job in the city. She will be ....."

Faith didn't wait to hear the rest of her mother's answer. Silently she closed her bedroom door.

Suddenly her door flew open and her father staggered in. "You hear that girl? You will end up just like Ethel. Don't even think about bringing your brats home for us to look after. You get pregnant, don't come running home to mom and dad all sorry like, expecting us to help you out. You won't get any help from us." Then he turned and lurched back into the hallway.

Faith was angry. He was giving her permission to leave but at what cost? Family whispers had always surrounded "poor Ethel" and her problem. Faith didn't know the whole story but nobody in the family had much to do with her. They felt she had disgraced them. Now, if anything she did reminded him of Ethel, she might as well not bother coming home. Her dad wasn't the kind who easily forgave people for their mistakes. Even the fact that she was his daughter wouldn't be enough to change his mind.

"You miserable so and so don't you worry. Once I leave, I am never coming back "she muttered to herself slamming the door shut behind him.

TWO

The next few days passed in a whirlwind of activity. Faith finished her exams and she and her mother made a trip to Lancaster apartment hunting but to no avail. Rent was high, the damage deposit and first month's rent were more than her parents could afford.

While in Lancaster she had an interview with Elizabeth Heatley, the personnel director for the firm of Northrup and Amos. She came across to Faith as stern and unnerving, quickly laying down the office rules and what she expected from her employees.

"You will notice everyone dresses professionally, skirts, or suits. Pant suits and pants with a jacket are allowed. When required to go to court you wear a business suit. No open toed shoes or sandals are allowed in court but you may wear them in the office. Definitely no jeans, flip flops or running shoes. If you are working on a weekend you are free to wear whatever you wish, unless you are representing the company. Our professional image is important to us." she added.

"You will be called to work upon a variety of projects, sometimes more than one at a time. You may be required to come in early and work late. If you are here in the office past eight o'clock, a taxi will be provided to take you home unless you have your own car.

Everything that takes place inside this office must be held in strictest confidence. You will be fired immediately if we prove you have divulged stories outside the firm. Every client is to be treated with dignity and respect when they walk through the doors. It's not up to us to decide if they are guilty or innocent. That decision lies with the court.

My last piece of advice is, try not to get personally involved. Most cases are routine, wills, estates and so on, but every once in a while a case will come along that will break your heart. Your job is to assist our lawyers in putting their best case forward. We also discourage fraternization between our employees because this invariably leads to problems. In fact, we have lost many good people for this very reason."

Faith didn't have any questions for her. This was the same information she had been taught in school.

"Good then," said Mrs. Heatley "we will see you here at eight o'clock the morning of the eleventh."

Recounting their conversation to her mother she exclaimed "I don't like her. She is bossy and I would hate to get on the wrong side of her. That old battle axe could make life really miserable if she wanted to."

In the end Faith and her mother settled on a room at the YWCA. The price was affordable and was located six blocks from the office tower where Faith would be working. Walking to work each morning meant she would save money on bus fare.

The room, similar to a motel room contained a single bed, a hide a bed sofa in case a friend stayed over, a desk, television set, and a chair. Across the back wall was a top cabinet with two doors, a small bar fridge underneath a stained counter top, a microwave and a two burner electric stove. A small but adequate bathroom was tucked into the corner along the same wall. Posted on the back of the door was a set of rules; no men were allowed in the rooms, no parties, no alcohol was allowed on the premises, lights off at eleven, a coin washer and dryer were available on each floor, and if staying out after midnight, a late pass was available from the front desk. Although this wasn't exactly what Faith had been looking for, she gave into her mother's pleas and agreed to stay until she could afford something better. Faith hated the idea of living by more rules but she could understand how they helped her mother feel better about leaving her.

Graduation day dawned warm and sunny. The ceremony was small, only she and her twenty classmates were graduating. Faith's mother had bought her a new yellow sun dress for the occasion. The graduates wore burgundy caps with a gold tassel and a burgundy gown. A small informal reception, sponsored by the school, took place afterwards. Their official formal graduation ceremony would be a part of the larger College Convocation that took place each fall. Faith was chosen as Valedictorian, and to her surprise, received a plaque and five hundred dollars for achieving the highest marks in her class. She had worried about her dad getting drunk and making a fool of them, but he was unusually quiet. Her mom cried, as she always did whenever anything sentimental came along.

Faith, found the ceremony anticlimactic. She was the envy of her friends and classmates, because she was the only student who had been accepted for a job.

After the reception Faith and her three closest girlfriends celebrated by going for supper. They formed a tight bond all through school but after tonight, each would be going her separate way. Chelsey, her best friend, was also hoping to get a job in the city. They were planning to share an apartment later on.

Faith was exuberant. "I can hardly believe I'm finally getting out of here. I was beginning to think this day would never come," she proclaimed.

"How is your dad taking the news about you leaving? I don't imagine he is very happy" one of the girls commented.

"Not very well" Faith replied. "I guess he'll just have to get used to the idea his little girl is all grown up and can look after herself. I do hate the idea of leaving my mother alone with him though. At least I could take some of the flak for her when I was home." Each one of them, having met Faith's father, knew what she meant.

Two days later Faith, her mother and father were moving her to Lancaster. The back seat and trunk of the small car were filled with boxes. Unsure of what she would need, Faith had packed everything she could think of; bedding, her computer, text books, her clothes, posters to hang on the walls, a coffee pot and some dishes. The cafeteria was open for breakfast and supper but closed at seven each evening. For the past week her mother had been filling and freezing plastic containers with cookies and individual meals for Faith to take with her.

"Mom you don't need to do that" Faith said. "I'll be fine. I won't starve and I am sure I'll have my first pay check within a short period of time."

"Hush girl" her mother retorted. "You don't have much money and everything in the city is very expensive. Besides, I want to do this for you."

When they finally arrived in front of the YWCA Clive Benson was pouting and refused to get out of the car. After trying for several minutes to coax him into coming to her room Faith and her mother left him sitting there. They packed the many boxes up two flights of stairs to her room and, within a short period of time, everything was put away and organized. With the addition of the posters, brightly colored drapes and a matching bedspread the room quickly lost its institutional look.

Once finished, they walked back to the car. "Be a good girl Faith" her mother said. "Work hard and go to church on Sunday. Be alert because anything can happen in the city."

"Don't worry mom. I'll be fine" Faith replied. "I'm a big girl, I can look after myself."

"Faith, you are entirely too trusting. If anything should happen you don't have any friends or family here to help you."

"Mom you worry too much. "

Upon their approach Clive Benson got out of the car. He put his arms around his daughter crushing her to his chest. He whispered into her ear "you don't have to do this you know. It's not too late to come back with us."

"I know dad. Try not to worry, I promise not to end up like Auntie Ethel."

He hugged her again then shoved something into her hand. Getting back into the car he drove away without looking back. Faith stood on the sidewalk waving until the car was out of sight, then she looked inside her hand to see what her father had given her. It was an envelope folded into four. Inside were a hundred dollar bill and a note which read. "I am proud of you. Keep this and use it in case you decide to come home. Dad."

She smiled softly to herself while thinking "He really wasn't that bad when he wasn't drinking."

She was up early the next morning. Wanting to make a good impression on her first day she chose her new emerald green suit to wear. The color set off her hazel eyes. She tied her long auburn hair back with a ribbon the same color as her suit and let it hang down her back. Underneath, she wore a cream colored short sleeve blouse which accentuated her pale porcelain skin. Inside her new brief case she put the sandwich and apple she prepared earlier for her lunch.

Walking slowly down the street, she absorbed the sounds of the traffic, the smell of the exhaust and the people scurrying past her. She noticed a small grocery store, a drug store and the smell of fresh bread wafting from a nearby bakery. She passed a small cafe where several older men were sitting outside, reading their newspapers and drinking their morning coffee. She smiled at the people who passed her. Some smiled back, most didn't.

She sighed with contentment, "I know I am going to be happy here, a new job, and a new place to live. How did I ever get so lucky? This is my world now and I am looking forward to being a part of this community."

Once again she was filled with awe as she saw her office building - Robinson Office Tower it was called. The building, fifty floors high was made of blue shimmering glass panels. In the early morning the sun shining on the panels reminded her of the prisms her mom hung in their kitchen window. Pulling open the heavy blue tinted glass doors she entered into an open spacious lobby. To her left was a sunken garden area filled with large plants, benches and small vibrantly colored tables with two chairs. It was prettier than any park back home. She quickly decided this was where she would come to eat her lunch every day.

The wall in front of her was an opaque glass water feature which fell from one of the higher floors. Various colored lights shone on the water as it snaked down the glass wall ending with a splashing sound into a small round pool. To her right was an information desk and beyond that a bank of eight elevators.

Walking up to the information desk she said to the older white haired man wearing a black security uniform. "Hello, my name is Faith Benson and this is my first day of work at the law firm of Northrup, Amos. Mrs. Heatley told me to check in with you when I got here."

"Hello Miss Benson. My name is Andrew. Yes, your name is on my list." Handing her a plastic card attached to long black ribbon he said "This is your temporary security card. We'll get you fixed up with a more permanent one later today. If there is anything you need, don't hesitate to ask.

This here card opens that side door over there and opens the elevators after hours. If you come in early or leave late you will need this. Security cameras help us track who is in the building so we can check on them if there is any kind of a problem. I lock the front doors when I leave at seven, and open them when I arrive at the same time in the morning. Sixteenth floor is where you are supposed to go want," he added.

Faith accepted the card from him, smiled then turned and walked into an open elevator. Taking a deep breath she pushed the button for the sixteenth floor.

When the door opened, Mrs. Heatley was waiting for her. Looking at her watch she remarked "Good morning Faith. Right on time I see. Andrew called to let me know you were on your way up. Come I will show you where you will be working."

Turning right from the elevators they stopped in front of the fourth office on the left hand side. "This is your office."

 The small drab room contained a desk, two chairs, a computer and a tired fake palm tree in the corner. There was also a small corner closet and a shelf along the wall behind the desk. There were no outside windows and a dusty white blind covered the large window facing the corridor.

Handing her a key, Mrs. Heatley said "You can add any personal touches that you wish to fix this room up, but most likely you won't spend much time in here. Come along now, there is more to see."

Faith trailed behind her like a puppy dog. "This wing also hosts the library, a staff conference room and the offices of the other four Legal Assistants. At the end of the hall way is the lunch room where we provide tea, coffee or juice. The washrooms are located there also. If you prefer to eat here there is a cafeteria in the basement"

Turning back, they once again arrived in front of the elevator and were standing at the reception desk. "Straight ahead are the private offices of Mr. Northrup and Mr. Amos. Their private secretary is Cecilia Owen." Mrs. Heatley pointed out.

"Behind this desk is Evelyn, our receptionist. Down that hallway behind her are the partners' offices and two client conference rooms. There are six partners working here and eight associates working out of our two sub-offices. You will meet them later. At one time or another they will show up wanting your help. You and the other Legal Assistants work with each partner. Nobody works exclusively with one unless I have assigned them to a specific case. Some of the partners you will find easier to work with than others. Two partners share a secretary and my advice is to get on their good side right away. Doing so will save you a lot of time and grief later. They tend to be territorial at times.

Evelyn, our receptionist is our miracle worker. Somehow she manages to keep us all organized. Frankly I don't know how she does it. If she ever decides to leave us I am positive we will fall apart. My office is located to your right. I have an open door policy. If you are unsure about how to proceed with anything come and check with me first. Better this than having to start all over again. Mistakes can be costly," she continued.

"Evelyn, please call Cassandra and ask her to come do Faith's orientation." Then, turning to Faith she said "you will be working with her for the next few days until you can find your way around. She will help you get settled in your office then take you to security for your pass."

Cassandra Evans was a tall heavily bleached very attractive blond. She wore a low cut too tight sweater which accentuated her cleavage and a tight blue skirt. She walked with a definitive sway in her hips.

"Come on honey," she said, "let's get you settled." Faith would soon learn she called everybody honey.

"See you got the lecture from the dragon lady on how to dress," referring to Faith's green suit. "She's not so bad but a real stickler for protocol. Me, I don't care what she says. I 'm only here until I meet a rich lawyer, retire in style and raise a bunch of kids. You'll be working with me until you get the hang of things. After that we will turn you loose on the big boys. You are beautiful and smart too I hear. You, honey, are going to knock their socks off."

Faith chuckled to herself. She immediately liked Cassandra and her saucy ways. The rest of the day was a blur of activity and meeting her co-workers. Faith wondered how she would ever get their names straight. She got her permanent security pass with her picture on the front, paper and supplies for her office, found how the library system was set up and tried to keep from getting lost or in the way.

Quickly she caught onto the office routine. At first she was given small tasks then, as her confidence grew, larger more demanding ones. Daily she walked to the court house to deliver papers and pick up court documents. She learned to check on land titles and more about wills and estates. Mrs. Heatley was always available to answer her questions, and then point her in the right direction.

Once or twice a week she travelled to the sub-offices to work with the associates. The atmosphere was fun and more relaxed. They were all young married professionals who worked hard and played equally hard, constantly competing against each other, but in a friendly way. Twice they had invited her for a barbecue on a Saturday evening and she had met their wives and children. She appreciated these invitations. They offered her an opportunity to get away from the YWCA and do something else besides work.

Faith looked forward to her weekends. On Saturday mornings she would shop at the small grocery store and visit the open air Farmers market. She sat outside the cafe and read the newspaper over lunch. In the afternoons she explored the parks and river front trails of the neighborhood. Some of the shop keepers began greeting her by name when she entered their store. This made her feel that she lived in as small town within the city and kept her from getting overly homesick.

Every Sunday morning she phoned her mother. After recounting all that happened during the week she asked "How is dad doing? Is he still mad at me for leaving?"

"I think so, but he doesn't say much. Most of the time he sits and drinks from the time he gets home until he goes to bed. Weekends are the worst," she added.

"Mom, why do you stay with him? Why do you continue to put up with his abuse? Come and live with me."

"Faith." her mother replied, "He is my husband and you know I don't believe in divorce."

Faith particularly enjoyed working in the accounting department. After discovering she had a knack for working with numbers Mrs. Heatley offered to pay for several night courses if she decided to specialize in that area. She and Cassandra became good friends at work. If their schedules permitted they ate lunch together. Once or twice, when they had both worked late, they had gone for supper.

"Faith" Cassandra said one day. "My roommate is moving out at the end of the month. How about moving out of the Y and into my place? We can share the rent and expenses. You can get away from that eleven o'clock curfew, and start to have a real life."

"The Y is convenient for me to walk to work. "Faith replied, "do you live much farther away? As it is, I walk six blocks every day,"

"My house is on Fifth Street, three blocks off this Avenue. Probably take you an extra five minutes or so."

She had been waiting for the right opportunity to move out of the Y and into her own place. Chelsey had accepted a job in town and wouldn't be moving to the city to share an apartment with her.

Faith was excited. This sounded too good to be true "I'm going to take you up on that offer. Tonight when I get back I'll give my two weeks' notice then I can move the first of the month. "

"Two weeks will be just fine honey. First of the month you and I will be roomies."

When she got back to the Y room that evening, she stopped at the front desk and gave her notice. She debated about calling and telling her mom, but decided not to.

"No" she said to herself. "I am a big girl now. I don't need their permission for every little thing I do, besides, Mom will try and talk me into staying here. I know she feels I am safer here but this place is boring."

THREE

The first of the month, a Saturday, arrived faster than Faith expected. Prior to moving she had spent time shopping for a new bed, dresser and desk at the local second hand store. When Cassandra and her friend arrived with a pickup truck to help her move she was packed, ready to go. One trip was all it took. Several hours later, she was settled into her new room.

The house was old and appeared quite dilapidated on the outside. Inside the rooms were freshly painted and had been renovated within the last few years. Her upstairs room was located on the east side where the early morning sun shone into her room. Across the hall was the bathroom and Cassandra's room. She was pleased that her room was considerably larger than the one she had at the YWCA

Within a short period of time her posters were up on the wall, the colorful drapes covered the window and her coordinating bedspread fit her new bed. The only piece of furniture she needed to buy was a chair for her desk. She planned to come up here if she brought work home from the office.

Faith felt slightly out of place as she joined Cassandra in the living room. She knew it was going to take a day or so before she was comfortable living in this new arrangement.

"I'm going to the Crown and Anchor Pub tonight, "Cassandra said. "Come with me, we will celebrate your moving in. Saturdays they have a live band and open up the dance floor. Usually it isn't hard to find someone to dance with. All you have to do is look like you are interested."

"I don't know Cassandra. I don't dance very well and I'm not much of a drinker. I think I'll just stay here tonight and finish getting settled. My dad was pretty strict, so I'm used to staying home on the weekends. He used to say as long as I lived in his house I followed his rules."

"Well your dad isn't here, is he? You can do whatever you want. Come on honey, it will be fun. Maybe we will meet a couple handsome rich guys. Who knows what could come from that."

Faith giggled when she heard this. The last thing on her mind was meeting a "handsome rich guy". She was enjoying her independence and life for the first time.

After much coaxing, Faith somewhat reluctantly agreed to go with Cassandra. "I guess one time won't hurt," she replied

The two of them went up to Faith's room to find something suitable for her to wear for the evening. She borrowed one of Cassandra's low cut beaded black sweaters and a pair of white jeans. Cassandra showed her how to apply a little makeup and fixed her hair.

Faith felt very self-conscious and out of place entering the Pub for the first time. She had been forbidden to go to bars with the rest of her friends and didn't know what to expect. When Cassandra opened the door loud music was pounding in the background. She saw a few bodies swaying on the dance floor. The flashing strobe lights added to her confusion. The din of people shouting to be heard was overwhelming.

Taking her by the hand, Cassandra steered her to a small round table half way into the room. Faith, unsure what was expected of her sat down there looking around. Cassandra ordered and paid for their drinks.

"Oh my Lord, this is more than what I expected. I see why you wanted to come here tonight," exclaimed Faith.

When their drinks arrived Faith tasted hers and said "What is this? It tastes really good."

"It's Sangria, made with wine and fruit juices."

Taking a big sip Faith said "tastes a little more like lemonade to me."

"Take it easy honey. They taste good but pack quite a punch," warned Cassandra.

The next morning, when Faith opened her eyes, her head was pounding and her stomach was churning. Snippets of the evening rushed through her mind. She remembered slow dancing with some guy on the dance floor, more drinks, Cassandra walking her into the house, throwing up into the toilet before falling asleep on the bathroom floor.

She vaguely remembered Cassandra putting her into bed and saying "Honey, you sure don't know how to hold your drinks very well. You are going to have to learn to pace yourself."

Slowly she crawled out of bed. The slightest movement increased the pounding in her head. She felt as if she was going to throw up. Eventually she showered and dressed, then slowly crept downstairs. Cassandra was watching a movie on TV.

"Honey" she said "You look like crap."

"I am really sick. I must have the flu or something. I don't remember ever feeling so terrible. I feel like I'm dying."

"That honey, is what they call a hangover. You were sure putting them away last night and that little French guy thought he was in for a good time."

"Oh no, did I make a fool of myself? How many drinks did I have anyway? The most I've drunk before last night was a little wine at Christmas. My dad drinks enough for all of us. Did I tell you know that was the first time I have been inside a bar?"

"Yes. You must have told me a dozen times last night. Sit here while I go and get something to help you feel better."

Cassandra got up off the couch, went to the kitchen and returned with a cup of coffee and two Tylenol. "Take these; you'll be fine in no time." Then more seriously she added "Honey you are going to have to learn to be more careful. I won't always be there to look after you That guy you were making out with on the dance floor had only one thing on his mind, and that was getting you out of there as fast as he could and into bed. You were heading out the door with him when I caught up to you. He wasn't very happy when I dragged you back inside."

"Never again Cassandra, never again," she said as she lay down on the sofa pulling a blanket up to her shoulders and closing her eyes..

The two girls fell into a routine. They worked hard during the week and played equally hard all weekend. Usually they started with the staff for Happy Hour on Friday night, slept late on Saturday then went back to the

Pub Saturday evening. Sometimes Cassandra would leave early with some guy she had met and Faith took a taxi home alone.

One Saturday night, they had barely sat down when Cassandra poked Faith in the arm. "See that guy over there. A month ago he was hired for the east side office and last week Mr. Amos moved him into the main office."

"I don't recall seeing him at either place" Faith said. "I certainly would have noticed him!"

"Trust me. When I saw him the first time, I made a point of finding out all about him. Handpicked by Mr. Amos, he is to be the future golden boy of our firm. The partners are expecting big things from him. Now that is the kind of guy I've been looking for."

Faith watched Lance Palmer circle the bar like a politician, talking to those he knew, shaking hands with those he was meeting for the first time. As he moved closer to their table Cassandra pushed herself away and walked over to him. Within minutes she had him by the hand and was leading him back to their table.

"Faith Benson, meet Lance Palmer. Lance was surprised when I told him we all work in the same office. I also told him you and I were the best Legal Assistants in the city, and if he ever needs assistance he should come to us first."

Faith blushed as he took her hand in his and solemnly said "Hello Miss Benson. I am always in need of a first class assistant." Holding her hand a little too long and too tightly he softly added "I look forward to working with both of you."

Faith watched him walk away. Tall with an athletic build, Lance Palmer was probably a good ten years older than she was. His strong muscular shoulders rippled under the white t-shirt he was wearing. His hair, streaked with touches of gray along the side, made him look distinguished. He also possessed the most beautiful blue eyes Faith had ever seen. An aura of confidence emanated from him.

Faith said to herself "wow, he is something else. That is the most handsome man I have met in my life." Her heart was still pounding from the touch of his hand upon hers.

Cassandra left with him. They chatted for a few minutes then she returned to their table.

"I'm in love," she said dreamily. "Isn't he the sexiest thing you have ever seen? He was asking about you, like how long have you worked at the office. He didn't remember seeing you there either. I think he's interested in you."

"Don't be so silly Cassandra. I'm not interested in getting mixed up with anybody right now. I want to get my career on track first."

Faith was quiet for the rest of the evening. Every time she glanced up Lance Palmer was staring at her, making her feel very uncomfortable

Finally she said to Cassandra "maybe we should call it a night. Not much going on here and I'm tired. Tough week I guess."

"Honey that guy keeps staring at you. Don't you want to wait and see what the rest of the evening brings? He looks like the type who enjoys having a good time."

"No. I just want to go home."

They finished their drinks then walked home unsteadily, giggling like a pair of school girls.

That night, when Faith went to bed, she couldn't get Lance Palmer off of her mind. Something about him electrified her. Since they worked in the same off ice it was inevitable they would meet again.

FOUR

A week later, Mrs. Heatley called Faith into her office. "Faith, I have an important assignment for you. One of our newest lawyers, Lance Palmer, is working on a multimillion dollar law suit and I want you to work with him."

"Mrs. Heatley, wouldn't it be a better idea if you chose one of the more experienced girls to work with him on this project? I'm not sure that I am ready yet to work on such a big case."

Mrs. Heatley, thinking that Faith was questioning her own abilities replied "No, I have been watching you and I know you are ready. Time you put all of your education to the test. Besides, he asked specifically for you, said that he had heard you were one of the best Legal Assistants in the firm. Besides you are the only one free, all of the others are tied up on cases right now."

Faith smiled weakly. "Damn that Cassandra and her big mouth. How can I work with someone who makes me feel the way he does? Yet, on the other hand if Mrs. Heatley wants me on this case, I really don't have a choice in the matter. That is what I am getting paid for."

"Good, that's settled" said Mrs. Heatley, "We have a meeting scheduled for nine tomorrow morning. Clear everything off your desk so you can devote yourself full time to this project. Winning this one is very important to the firm."

Faith worked late into the evening finishing off the projects she had started. She was happy Cassandra was already in bed when she got home. She didn't want to explain any details to her. Besides, she couldn't shake off that nagging doubt in the back of her mind. Her little voice was telling her not to get involved, to go back to Mrs. Heatley and request that she give the job to somebody else; someone better suited to deal with Lance Palmer.

The next morning Mrs. Heatley, Mr. Amos, Lance, herself, a secretary and two other staff lawyers, Connie Pierce and Lloyd Thomas met in the conference room. Faith took careful notes of what was said and the direction they were going to pursue.

Their client, Molly Brown, was suing General hospital for negligence. Her child had been given a wrong medication. Now he was brain damaged and would require full time care for the rest of his life. She was suing for fifty million dollars and ongoing support for the care of her son. The firm's fee was ten percent, or five million dollars.

After the meeting Faith felt differently. She was excited to be part of the legal team that was going to make a difference in this baby's quality of life.

The first weeks were grunt work. Faith spent most of her time looking up precedents, sitting in on interviews, office meetings and finding out all she could about the two medications involved. She had seen Lance enter the Pub with a very attractive blond hanging on his arm and couldn't believe how jealous she felt.

One evening she confided her feelings to Cassandra. "I am falling in love with him. Each day I wait for him to show up at the office. Then I am sitting on pins and needles until he calls me for some reason. I love being with him. I don't want to get mixed up with him, I know that he is much too old and too sophisticated for me, but I can't help myself."

"Honey, be careful." Cassandra said seriously. "You are playing with fire and could end up getting hurt. He's not the right guy for you. This sort of thing happens all the time. When we are working closely with someone it's easy to think we feel an attraction and no wonder. You are both deeply involved, spending a lot of time together, sharing the highs and lows, in effect your lives center around the case. Then, when it's over you both go in your separate directions. The next time you meet, you wonder what you ever saw in that person. Take it from someone who knows" she said bitterly, "been there, done that."

"But."

"I know honey, but he's a player. I have heard a few things around the office about him and most of them were uncomplimentary. You don't need guys like that in your life. Behind those great looks is a real loser."

Faith listened to Cassandra half-heartedly. All the while she was thinking "she is jealous because it's me working with him not her."

The closer they came to the court date, the more time she put in at the office. Once again, they were working late into the evening, building a flow chart to demonstrate the sequence of events at the hospital that fateful evening. Another very sick baby had been admitted and the hospital ward was short staffed. One nurse, trying to do the work of three, unintentionally mixed up the medications. It shouldn't have happened but the two bottles looked exactly the same, and one had accidentally been placed in the wrong spot. In her haste, the nurse had not read the label properly.

They were standing side by side, following the events of the evening to make sure they hadn't missed anything, when Lance reached down, turned her face toward him and kissed her gently on the lips. When he released her, Faith looked up into his blue eyes and didn't know what to say.

He smiled at her and said "I have wanted to do that ever since that night I met you at the Pub. You are a beautiful woman Faith. You are everything I have been searching for."

Faith continued staring at him. Surely he could hear her heart beating like a drum in her chest. She wanted to throw herself into his arms and kiss him again but instead she said "I have to go."

Grabbing her purse from the desk top, she scurried from the room like a frightened little mouse. His kiss had taken her off guard. She could still feel his touch on her skin. Suddenly she didn't know what to do. Should she go back into the room and pretend nothing happened or go home? Standing there in the hallway she could hear him whistling to himself on the other side of the door. She went home.

In the morning she was embarrassed by her over reaction to the kiss the night before. After tossing and turning most of the night, she decided to try and find the right words to explain to him that her career came first and she wasn't interested in getting involved in a relationship with someone from the office. She was enjoying her life just the way it was.

Faith didn't have an opportunity that day, or the next to be alone with Lance, to explain herself and state her intentions. Their case had gone to trial and was in the middle of jury selection. They were all busy with last minute details.

Then, one Wednesday morning he casually asked her "would you mind staying late tonight? I know you may have plans and I apologize, but there are a couple of details I want to go over to make sure I have them clear."

A few minutes after five she knocked on Lance's office door and walked in. "He looks tired" she thought. He was bent over his desk sorting through a very large pile of paper.

"Glad you are here. I need you to double check the birth records of that baby. See if there were any problems. Our worthy opponent is claiming the baby was born brain damaged - some sort of genetic anomaly. They are claiming that, because he had an undetected condition and was already brain damaged, the medication didn't cause his problem. Our job is to prove he was a healthy baby until that day. Tomorrow see if there is any chance the cord blood was saved. Check with the mom. If she isn't sure, call the hospital. If so, then arrange to have the sample tested at a private lab for genetic problems. They can send the bill to the office. If not, they are going to have a hard time proving their point. I also want you to double check the precedents we are using to be sure we haven't missed anything."

Several hours later Lance looked up from his papers and announced "I'm hungry. How about you? When did you eat last?"

"I skipped lunch today," Faith confessed. "I was over at the east side office until late this afternoon. Sometimes when I am busy I forget to eat."

"Grab you coat and let's go. I know a really great place not too far from here. Hope you like pasta, we can finish the last of this in the morning."

"Sounds like a good idea to me."

Faith went to her office, grabbed her coat and purse. Stopping in the washroom she refreshed her make up and took out the pony tail clip allowing her hair to hang loosely past her shoulders and frame her face. Lance was waiting for her at the elevator.

"I like your hair that way," he said.

Soon they were sitting at a table for two in a dimly lit Italian restaurant. She ordered Fettuccine and a glass of wine. He ordered a steak and a double rye whiskey and water.

Conversation flowed easily between them. At first they talked about the case but after her third glass of wine Faith was telling him about her dad and home town. She was doing most of the talking and failed to notice that Lance was on his fifth drink.

"Look Faith, I need to stop at my place first and pick up some papers I forgot this morning, then I will take you home. Do you mind? After I drop you off, I'm going back to the office for a couple of hours."

"Fine with me" Faith replied.

As he was parking the car in his underground parking stall he suggested "why don't you come up with me? I have the most beautiful view of the city from my window. Besides I don't think it's safe to leave you here alone."

"No thank you, I don't mind waiting here. I'll be fine; I promise to keep the doors locked until you get back."

"Come on, it will only take five minutes. I promise to be a good boy."

Faith laughed although she wasn't sure what he meant by his last remark. She felt uncomfortable riding in the elevator. She had never been invited to a man's apartment before. Alarm bells were ringing in her head but she ignored them, preferring the warm fuzzy feeling from the wine.

Lance's apartment was breath taking. It was only one large room with a black tempered glass circular stairway in the middle leading to a loft upstairs. To her left were a small compact kitchen and a dining area containing a smoky gray glass table and four chairs. Dark hardwood floors contrasted perfectly with the stark white walls. The only other pieces of furniture were a black leather sofa and matching chair in front of the window and a large flat screen television set that hung from the ceiling. A large white pile rug lay in front of the sofa. The walls were attractively decorated with a wide variety of colorful paintings. Behind the stairs Faith noticed a small powder room

He was right. The view of the city from this window on the twenty-first floor was spectacular. She could see the twinkling city lights below framed by the blackness of the country side beyond. The only sound in the room was her breathing.

Lance interrupted her contemplative mood when he came up behind her and put both hands around her waist. "Beautiful isn't it" he said.

"Yes" she replied, and then turned, stood on her tip toes and kissed him on the cheek. "Thank you for a wonderful evening" she whispered.

With a moan he swept her into his arms and began kissing her passionately. She tried to pull away but he held her tightly. Her conscience was urging her to make him stop, but her body was responding otherwise. Breathlessly she gave into the demands of his lips. She had never felt like this before. Slowly, while still kissing her, he slipped off her suit jacket then unzipped the back of her slacks, pushing them past her hips to the floor. Then he reached between them and began unbuttoning her blouse.

"No Lance." she whispered against his lips. "Please stop. I have never....."

He kissed her protests away as he slowly and effortlessly lowered her to the floor holding her with one arm, removing the last of her clothing with his other hand. She was lost in his embrace, the gentleness of his touch and the passion that was consuming her. She gasped when he entered her. He stopped, laying on top of her whispering endearments into her ear.

Slowly she reached up, put her hands on his hips and whispered "don't stop," then gave into the crashing waves of never before felt emotions. Everything seemed so natural; it was as if they were meant to be together.

Afterwards they lay on the white rug in front of the window, the city lights sparkling beneath them. Her head was resting on his shoulder.

"Am I your first?" he murmured into her hair.

"Yes" she said huskily. In his hands, and in less than ten minutes, she had changed from a girl to a woman.

"Thank you" he said. She looked up at him and he began kissing her again. It was as if their hungry bodies couldn't get enough of the other. They satisfied themselves again and again.

Finally Faith said. "Lance I have to go home some time tonight."

"Stay here with me," he pleaded.

"I can't. Cassandra will be wondering what happened to me," she said reaching for her clothes. "I thought you had to go back to the office."

"May be later, for now you go and get dressed and I'll call you a taxi" he said.

Self-consciously she picked her clothes up off the floor and walked naked to the powder room. Lance was dressed waiting for her when she came out, a smirk of satisfaction on his face.

Walking hand in hand they went down the elevator and waited by the entrance for the taxi to arrive. They stood there kissing each other good night over and over again. Running his hands up and down her body he begged her to come back up upstairs to his apartment. When the taxi pulled up he opened the door for her, paid the driver then kissed her on the cheek. "I'll see you tomorrow." he whispered huskily in her ear.

Faith couldn't go to sleep. Silent tears flowed down her cheeks as she recalled the feeling of his hands on her. She was ashamed for acting so wanton, but at the same time was feeling fulfilled as a woman. Instinctively she knew that she had crossed a threshold into a new world and would never be able to go back. Her life, as she knew it, would never be the same again.

Lance was in court the rest of the week which suited Faith just fine. She was embarrassed and humiliated for giving into his demands so easily. The next time she saw him he was escorting the same blond into the pub. Her heart skipped a beat. He spotted her, smiled and waved, then turned his attention back to his girlfriend.

Faith sat there as long as she could and then started to cry. Cassandra glanced at her weeping friend then at Lance, and immediately understood what was going on.

"Come on honey. Let's get you home."

By the time they walked back to the house Faith had stopped crying. Cassandra went into the kitchen and made a pot of coffee, Faith sat in the living room staring at the wall. When the coffee was ready she brought a cup to Faith.

"OK honey; tell me what this is all about."

Faith looked at her friend sadly. "I slept with him. He was my first." She told Cassandra about going to his apartment, and how one little kiss of gratitude had turned into her first sexual experience.

"Cassandra, I've never had a real boyfriend. Dad wouldn't let me go out with boys. I have only been kissed once before and it sure wasn't like that.

"How could I have been so naive and stupid? The first time a man kisses me I can't say no and mean it. Instead, I can't get enough of him. When he touched me I felt a heat rise up within me and I wanted him as badly as he wanted me. Does being in love with him make my behavior acceptable? I was saving myself for my husband and our wedding night. When I saw him tonight with that blond I felt like such a fool, like another one of his conquests."

When she was finished ranting Cassandra sighed. "What's done is done. What you experienced is not love honey, that was plain old fashioned lust. You can't undo what happened that night. Is there any chance that you might have gotten yourself pregnant?"

"No. I know for a fact I'm not" Faith replied.

"Good. Tomorrow we are going to get you to a clinic for some birth control pills."

"Cassandra, I don't think so" she protested. "My religion doesn't permit any kind of contraception. If my parents found out I was taking the pill, they would disown me. Besides I have no intention of ever having sex with him again. From now on, when I say no, I will mean No."

"You will honey. If you think you are in love with him the rest is inevitable. In the meantime we have to make sure you are protected. Same thing happened to me. I ended up giving my baby away for adoption. Take it from me, you don't want to have to go through an ordeal like that. It nearly killed me."

The next morning Cassandra took her to a Walk in Clinic and Faith came away with a prescription for birth control pills. After getting it filled, they spent a lazy afternoon having lunch and going shopping. Cassandra bought two sweaters that should have been two sizes bigger. Faith augmented her meager wardrobe with a new pant suit and pink sweater.

Later that evening Cassandra asked "Are you coming to the Pub with me tonight?"

"No, I think I'll just stay here."

"Look Faith, you need to stop beating yourself up for being human. You made a mistake, we all do at some time, but life goes on. Chalk it up to experience and stop feeling sorry for yourself. Besides you can't hide from him forever. You are still working in the same office and on the same case. You are bound to run into each other at one time or another.

"I know Cassandra but I don't feel like being around a bunch of people tonight. You go ahead without me."

FIVE

If fate had not intervened, Faith may have been able to avoid being alone with Lance, but such was not the case. He won the law suit against the hospital and the firm had a five million dollar pay day. Champagne flowed like water as everybody on staff, including Faith celebrated.

Feeling slightly tipsy she staggered to her office to get her purse and coat. It was time to go home, but when she opened the door Lance was sitting on the corner of her desk   with a full bottle of champagne and two empty glasses.

"You and I make a good team. Come, we need to have a celebration drink" he slurred, filling both two glasses and handing one to her. They raised their glasses in a toast. "To more victories." he said.

Faith gulped the champagne down and said. "I'm going home, I've had more than enough to drink tonight."

Unsteadily she moved to walk past him to the closet, but he grabbed her around the waist and pulled her closer to him.

"Come home with me Faith. I need you."

Every promise that she made to herself to stay away from him dissolved with his touch. She turned, kissing him passionately. His hands were all over her - his kiss taking her breath away.

Throwing caution to the wind she replied "Let's get out of here now."

Lance helped her on with her coat. "Go downstairs and wait for me. I need to get my laptop and will meet you there. Best we aren't seen leaving together."

Faith did exactly as she was told.

She didn't go home that night or the next. They spent the weekend in bed together drinking champagne and making love. A new magical world opened for Faith. Lance was an expert lover, under his tutelage she was a fast learner. He did things to her that she had never imagined and evoked feelings she never dreamed were possible.

After that weekend, they spent all of their free time together. On Friday, after work, she would go to his apartment then, on Sunday, go back to Cassandra's.

They would walk along the river together holding hands; sharing kisses under the streetlights. Sometimes they would go to a movies sit in the back row and make out like teenagers. Other times, they would lie on the white rug looking out over the lights of the city below.

Lance was very romantic. She would find tiny gifts on her pillow, or one rose sitting on her desk. They tried to keep up their professional appearances at the office, but often stole kisses when they were alone. Lance was everything she dreamed about in a man, and every day she fell deeper in love with him. Sometimes, when he was sleeping, she would watch him breathe wondering how she had been so lucky to find her soul mate. If he asked, she would have willingly spent the rest of her life trying to keep him happy.

One Saturday morning he handed her a glass of champagne and dropped a small pink pill into it. "Faith I have something amazing I want you to try." he said holding the glass out to her.

"No. Lance, you know that I'm not into drugs. You are the only drug I need."

"Please Faith" he coaxed, "just this one time. Do it for me. Trust me. I wouldn't give you anything that would hurt you."

She wanted to refuse, but seeing the disappointment on his face she took the glass from his hand and drank it down.

The rest of the weekend was a blur. Later, when she tried to recall the events, she couldn't remember anything. In fact, she was never completely sure what had taken place over the past twenty four hours.

When she woke up Sunday afternoon, there were abrasions around her wrists and bite marks on her breasts. She felt dazed, confused and was alone. She remembered drinking several more glasses of champagne and Lance insisting he add more of the pink pills to them. She had been powerless to refuse. Disturbing memories of a video camera flashed through her mind but didn't make any sense. Dismissing these thoughts from her head she recalled his words 'I wouldn't do anything that would hurt you.'" She believed him.

She was relaxing in the tub when she heard him come into the apartment. Wrapping her wet body in a white fluffy towel she went downstairs. The table was set, coffee was perking and Lance was cooking bacon and eggs.

"Here" he said, "you look like you need something to eat" filling a plate and putting it down in front of her. She sat there in her towel eating breakfast, as if this was an everyday occurrence in her life.

Then she asked "Lance, what happened? I have bruises and bite marks all over me and I can't remember how they got there. As a matter of fact, I don't remember much since yesterday. What was that you kept insisting upon putting into my glass of champagne?"

Ignoring her question he answered "you had better get dressed. While you are doing that I will call a taxi to take you home." Then kissing her on her bare shoulder he said "you are one little hell cat in bed. Now you're mine, I own you."

She left the apartment by herself. For the first time since they had been together Lance hadn't offered to go downstairs with her.

When she finally did get home Cassandra looked at her and shook her head sadly. "Faith, you look like hell. I hope you know what you have gotten yourself into. "

After that weekend Faith began spending all of her nights with Lance. Their appetite for each other was insatiable. Every night was new experience. Sometimes they stayed home, other times they went to a party or club. She did whatever he asked, trying to live up to his expectations of her. Most mornings she woke up with a dull headache and dark circles under her eyes from not getting enough sleep. Other mornings she felt like she was still half drunk and drank black coffee while getting ready for work, some days she didn't go at all, and never bothered phoning

"Faith," Lance suggested one night. "I want you to move in here on a permanent basis. I want to see you lying beside me every night. I don't want to share you with any one especially Cassandra. I don't think she likes me very much."

"Are you asking me or telling me?" Faith replied teasingly.

"Take it any way you want" he retorted. Faith didn't recognize the sarcasm in his voice.

She was in love. Hearing these words made her feel that now her life was complete. The next day she moved everything into his apartment, setting up her bed in the spare room.

Cassandra tried to talk her out of moving but to no avail. "Faith, please don't do this" she pleaded. "You are throwing your life away. He doesn't love you, he is using you. Lance is not the man you think he is."

"Leave me alone Cassandra and stop telling me what I should or shouldn't do. He wants me there and I want to be with him."

"Honey he is going to hurt you big time. Please Faith, stop and think this over. It's all happening too fast."

"I know what I am doing. What you think doesn't matter. I belong to him now," she replied angrily. "Besides how I live my life is none of your business."

Soon after she moved in Lance began to change. Their drinking became heavier, the parties wilder. Lance demanded more from her. Now that all of her restrictions were gone, Faith matched his passion for love and life.

One evening at the Pub, when she was very drunk, she ran into Cassandra in the Ladies room. Cassandra looked at her with pity in her eyes.

"Faith, you are a wreck. Look at you, so drunk you can barely stand up. You have to quit abusing yourself like this night after night."

Faith stared back at Cassandra through bleary eyes and retorted "Why? Quit so that you can have him. He loves me and I love him." Then she lurched out.

Cassandra, with concern written all over her face, watched her friend leave. This was like watching a horror movie. She knew this was a disaster waiting to happen and was powerless to stop it.

Leaving the Pub early Lance and Faith went to a private party at one of the night clubs downtown where one of Lance's friends had rented a private room for the evening. Shortly after they arrived Lance disappeared and she went looking for him. She found him in a back room office with two other lawyers from the firm, lines of cocaine laid out on the table in front of each of them.

Lance looked up and saw her. "Come on baby, you got to give this a try."

"I would rather not. You know drugs aren't my thing," Faith protested.

"Come on, just once. You don't know what you're missing. Once won't hurt you. Come, I'll show you what to do."

Faith followed his directions, and that night cocaine became part of their routine party habits. She loved the invincible feeling the drug gave her. That first night they made love wilder and more passionately than ever before.

Soon Lance was openly using drugs in the evenings on a daily basis. Faith restricted her use to the weekends. He became more irritable and more aggressive. Sometimes, when he was high, he would force her into doing things that left her feeling used and degraded. If she objected too strenuously, he would twist her arm behind her back and leave bruises on her. She wanted to talk to Cassandra and ask her for advice, but since that evening at the Pub, their relationship had been strained. She had no one else to turn to for help.

Sometimes they were both high for an entire weekend. Faith stopped being careful about taking her birth control pills. They stopped making love and were fighting all the time. Their relationship was falling apart, and getting high or drunk seemed to be the only thing they had in common.

One Thursday morning when Faith stepped off the elevator Mrs. Heatley was waiting for her. She was sick, hung over and it had taken all of her energy to get up and go into work that morning.

"Faith, come into my office" she commanded.

"Faith followed her, sat down and Mrs. Heatley closed her office door. "I'm afraid we are going to have to let you go. Please go to your office and collect your things. I will call security to escort you out of the building."

Faith looked at her dumbly. "What? Why?"

"Look at yourself. The girl we hired was sharp, a good worker. She was interested in what she was doing and gave everything her best. You have become a drug addled drunk and we don't need your kind on our staff. Take a good look in the mirror, I guarantee you won't be proud of what you see, Not only that, we can't depend on you, We don't know if you will finish your projects or even show up for work when you are needed. It is eight o'clock in the morning and you look like you haven't been to bed yet. Aren't those the same clothes you were wearing yesterday?" then she paused before asking "Do you have anything you want to say for yourself before I call security?"

Faith looked at her and pleaded "please don't fire me? I really need this job. I'm sorry; I didn't mean to let this happen." The truth was she was wearing the same clothes as the day before. She had passed out at a party and hadn't even brushed her teeth before coming to work.

"What do you think we should do with you? I can't have you coming to work like this every day. You are a disgrace. What would your parents think? Take a minute to think about this while I get you a cup of coffee and get you half sober. I want you to remember why you lost your job."

Faith sat there staring at the floor, wishing she were dead. "How had everything so good turned bad so quickly?" Then she heard the echo of her dad's voice. "You are going to end up just like Ethel." Straightening her back in the chair and trying to comb her unruly hair with her fingers she replied to him "No I am not."

Mrs. Heatley returned with two steaming mugs of black coffee. Faith took hers gratefully. "Mrs. Heatly do you think you can give me another chance? I promise I will get myself straightened out. Please?"

There was something about seeing Faith sitting there, begging to keep her job that tore at Elizabeth Heatley's heart. She had faced this many times during the years she had worked at the firm; young girls filled with

44

promise and hope losing their way, some destroying their lives forever. Faith was different She was special and she didn't want to lose her.

"I have to think about this. Go get yourself cleaned up and presentable. You can go help Carole in accounting today. She's a little backed up with her filing."

After Faith left, she sat there thinking for a long time. Normally she wouldn't have hesitated or even considered keeping a girl in her condition on staff, but there was vulnerability about Faith, something that told her that she needed protection, that someone needed to watch out for her. This girl had the potential to go far. Against her better judgment, she decided to give her one more chance by putting her on probation for three months. That would give her time to prove herself one way or the other. If she was serious about keeping her job, she would pull herself together.

At noon Mrs. Heatley knocked on Faith's office door and walked in. She could see that Faith's eyes were red from crying, but her physical appearance was much improved. Her hair was combed into a neat pony tail; she had changed into a different sweater and applied a little make up.

"Faith, I have decided to put you on probation for next three months. If, for any reason you fail to complete your duties or miss work without permission or come drunk or high you will be dismissed. Now go home. Decide what you want to do with your life. You can keep on the way you are going or begin making grown up decisions. You're not a child any more, you are an adult. This decision is going to determine the rest of your life. It's up to you."

"You won't be sorry Mrs. Heatley," Faith promised.

When she returned to the apartment the first thing Faith did was mix a stiff drink and gulp it down. She needed that, but as soon as the fiery liquor hit her stomach she was running for the bathroom. For the next while she was violently ill. When her retching subsided she went back downstairs. Wrapping herself in a blanket she lie down upon the sofa and fell asleep.

Hours later she awoke. Her head felt clearer than it had for a long time. She made herself a sandwich and sat on the sofa staring at the lights of the city beneath her, waiting for Lance to come home. She wanted to talk this over with him and let him know that her job was more important than partying every night.

Still feeling felt hurt and angry, she knew deep down that Mrs. Heatley was right. Her life was spiraling out of control and she didn't know how to make it stop. She was being offered an opportunity to regain her self-esteem and she was going to take it.

The next morning she got up early and spent extra time getting ready for work. It was hard. Her hands were shaking; she was nauseous and light headed. What she wanted more than anything was a drink. She forced herself to eat a slice of toast, and then threw it back up. She wondered, "How can Lance do this night after night and still be able to function the next day?"

She arrived at work on time, still feeling shaky and spaced out. Mrs. Heatley saw her as she got off the elevator but said nothing. The girl was going to try. She hoped she would make it. Maybe she was not a lost cause after all.

During the next three days Faith felt like she was going through hell. She needed a drink more than she needed drugs. In the evenings she paced the floor, every fiber of her body crying out to be filled with alcohol. Many times she stood holding the liquor bottle in her hands but didn't take a drink. Lance usually didn't come home until after she was in bed so she still hadn't been able to talk to him. Several times she heard him stumbling in during the small hours of the morning then pretended to be asleep when he reached for her. On the morning of the fifth day she realized she had stopped shaking. She felt more grounded and more in tune with her surroundings than she had felt in a long time.

That Friday evening when they went to the Pub, Lance scoffed at her for ordering ginger ale. "What's with you tonight acting like miss goody two shoes?"

"I might have to work tomorrow." she lied. "The dragon lady called me up on the carpet said I wasn't paying enough attention to my job."

This was neither the time nor the place to go over the conversation. She wanted Lance sober when she talked to him. Now, she could see he was in worse shape than she was. Maybe she could convince him to slow down too.

Before the evening was over she gave up her good intentions and accepted a drink from Lance so he would quit bullying her. She told herself that she could stop anytime she wanted. After the pub closed they went to a party with some of Lances friends. She wanted to go home. She was tired of his taunts, his ridicule of her good intentions. Convincing herself that he would stop, she went along with him.

Faith was unable to resist the lure of the drugs that evening, but no matter how hard she tried, she couldn't get back the feeling of being high. In fact, she barely remembered getting home. What she did remember made her feel sick to her stomach.

She had been the only female at the party; Lance had started the chant when she took off her jacket. Take it off baby he had said. She remembered doing a strip tease on the coffee table, the men cheering and egging her on. One of them, she couldn't remember which one, grabbed her by the waist and began slow dancing with her, grinding his hips against hers. She remembered having sex with the some guy on the sofa with Lance slitting on the floor watching. She could remember him running his finger up and down the outside of her thigh, urging them on until she lost control and was screaming in ecstasy. Lance pushed the guy off, and then was on top of her as the others watched. She remembered that shortly after he finished, he threw her clothes at her and told her to get dressed. She wanted to stay but he insisted they leave. She realized that he had enjoyed watching her make a fool of herself. In fact his encouragement and hands pushed her emotions over the edge.

"When he saw what was going on why didn't he take me home? Why did he let me continue putting on that disgusting display? This is a new low even for me "she admitted to herself," I have done some disgusting things before to keep him happy, but nothing like this. Oh God, what was I thinking?"

Faith woke up early before Lance, put on her housecoat, crept quietly downstairs and stood at the window looking out over the city. Rain was falling and the gray sky reflected the heavy laden feeling in her heart.

She felt dirty and betrayed. She kept asking herself "why didn't he step in and put an end to the whole situation. If he really loved me how he could he allow another man to have sex with me while he watched? I think the best thing for both of us would be for me to leave today. I don't want to, but there is no way after last night that he will want me to stay."

Self-loathing filled her body. For the first time she saw where her new life had taken her, and it made her feel sick. "Mrs. Healy was right; I am a drug addled drunk. In my own way I am worse than Aunt Ethel ever was."

Lance was awake when she went back to their bedroom. She sat down beside him on the bed, tears running down her face.

"We need to talk" she said, between sobs, "I am so sorry about last night. I didn't mean to embarrass you in front of your friends like that. If you want, I will pack up my clothes and leave."

She expected to be yelled at, vilified or called names. Whatever he said to her she felt she had coming. She certainly didn't expect what he said next.

"Baby, "he said." you didn't hurt my feelings last night, in fact you really turned me on. I never knew that watching you have sex with another man would be such a mind blowing experience. We will have to try that again, but next time I will join in, none of this one at time stuff. I have always wondered what that would be like. I bet for a few bucks we all could have a good time. The boys weren't too happy when I took you out of there. They each thought they deserved to be next"

Then, against her protests he took her fiercely. She cried out as waves of pleasure crashed through her body. Before abandoning herself to him she told herself "He does love me." Somehow his suggestion failed to register in her mind. He had forgiven her that was all that mattered. Everything was going to be fine.

While eating lunch she had the opportunity to tell him about her conversation with Mrs. Heatley.

"She had no right to talk to you that way. Honey, you do whatever you want to do. If last night and this morning are any indication of what you want, I'm all for it." he said to her.

Ignoring his comment Faith said "Lance, let's get married. We are meant to be together. We can build a good life, have a couple of kids and get away from this rat race. The only thing I want in this world is to be your wife."

"Is that what you really want "he said, coming around the table nuzzling her neck.

"Yes," she answered breathlessly. Was Lance going to propose to her?

"I see. Well, that's not what I want! I want my wife to be pure and clean, not someone who is willing to sleep with any man who looks at her. You, my dear are a first class slut. You are the last person I would think of marrying. You showed me who you really were last night. I want you for a good time, and I don't intend to spend the rest of my life with someone the likes of you."

Faith had never felt so dirty in her life. She proposed to him and he had turned her down. At that moment, she wished she had listened to Cassandra. Later, when she thought back to his comment earlier in the morning, she realized he was serious. She meant nothing to him. She was nothing but a toy. If he could make money on her he would. He didn't love her. He was amusing himself, using her to live out his fantasies.

This knowledge hurt her deeply, "Maybe if I straighten out, quit drinking and doing drugs he will see who I am and learn to love me back." she told herself. "I have to try."

After than night Faith gave up drugs and drinking. Life went from bad to worse. Lance didn't come home for days at a time. When he was home they argued. He was constantly belittling everything she did.

She apologized over and over again, trying to make him understand that the drugs and alcohol had made her act that way, that's not who she really was. She begged his forgiveness, but he kept throwing that night back into her face.

One day, after one of their shouting matches, he said. "Get out. When I get home in the morning I don't want to see your ugly face around here."

"I am not going any place. I pay my share of rent on this apartment, clean your house, wash your clothes and screw you. How do you figure you can get along without me? Please Lance, don't do this to me. I love you."

He walked over and slapped her across the face. "Don't you ever talk to me like that again. When I say get out, I mean get out. I don't want to see you here when I get home" Then he left.

Faith was stunned. This was the first time he had slapped her. She was used to his angry outbursts, even the bruises he sometimes left on her arms, but this was further than he had gone before. Tomorrow he would come around apologizing, begging for forgiveness and she knew that she would forgive him.

They reached an uneasy truce. For a short period of time he came home from work every night. They would have supper together, then sit and work on their individual lap tops. Gradually Faith let her defenses down. She reassured herself by saying "I'm sure hitting me was an accident. He didn't mean to hurt me. He said he was sorry and I have forgiven him. That's the end of it."

Her fantasy blew up in her face a week later. Lance, once again, started coming home later and later. She believed him when he claimed he was working late. After winning that big law suit, he was Mr. Amos' golden boy. The firm gave him every choice assignment that came along. The talk around the office was that they were considering offering him a full partnership,

Faith's life has she knew it changed that fateful day she came home early from work and decided it was a good opportunity to get the laundry done. Bending down to pick up Lance's dirty shirt off the floor to put into the laundry hamper she noticed a red mark on the collar. Taking a closer look, she realized it was lipstick. In his front pocket was a note. "L. I can't wait to see you again tonight. J"

Faith felt like she had been punched in the stomach. Who was J and how long had this been going on. She was angry. While waiting up for him to come home she rehearsed what she was going to say. She told herself "I have had enough. In the morning I am leaving for good."

As soon as the door opened she snapped, "It's about time you got home."

"What are you still doing up" he slurred, "thought you would be in bed by now."

"Who the hell is J.?" She demanded, throwing the note in his face.

"None of your business!"

"Here I am serving as your maid and housekeeper, and you are out screwing around with another woman. Who the hell do you think you are? "

Lance grabbed her around the throat with one hand, and punched her in the face with the other. Then he threw her on the floor.

Faith got back up to her feet and slapped him back. "I told you never to hit me again. The first time was the last time. I am out of here."

Grabbing her by the wrist he said "You aren't going any place. You will do what I tell you, when I tell you. Don't you ever talk to me in that tone of voice again. For your information, I invited the boys over on Friday and I have plans for you. I promised them you would be their entertainment. They are paying me two hundred bucks each for the privilege so you had better damn well accommodate them. A little booze and some drugs and it will be easy for you."

"Are you crazy? There is no way in hell I will do that for you, so you had better get that fantasy out of your head because it isn't going to happen. I won't prostitute myself to give you a thrill. You are real a pig. I never realized it before."

She turned to walk up the stairs. He grabbed her long hair and pulled her backwards. She landed with a thump at his feet. She fought him with everything she had, but he was taller and stronger. He kicked her, then grabbed her by the hair and began dragging her around the room bouncing her head off the walls and the floor.

Faith was scared. She had never seen him so violent. "Lance, stop" she screamed. Maybe that would bring him to his senses. "Stop you're hurting me. I'm sorry. I'll do whatever you want."

He didn't seem to hear her. She managed to get to her feet but he pulled her down again, and then kicked her in the side, taking her breath away. At one point, she tried to run into the kitchen to get the phone and call the police, but he smashed it out of her hand. Then he grabbed her and threw her head first into the wall. Faith was positive he was trying to kill her.

When he stopped to catch his breath, she ran into the living room and up the stairs. She thought "if I can get to the bathroom I'll lock myself in there until he calms down." She tried closing the door but he hurled himself against it. He grabbed her by the hair again and forced her down to her knees in front of him.

"You can't make me do that. Please Lance, you are hurting me."

"Didn't bother you before," he sneered. "If I recall correctly you kind of like it. In fact I think I have a video that tells the real story."

He pulled off his belt, unzipped his pants and pushed them down. When she refused, he began whipping her across her back and shoulders. Finally she stopped moving, there was no place to go. She stared up at him defiantly. Then he yanked her to her feet by her hair, flipped her backwards onto the floor, tore her clothes off, and violently raped her. She laid there, the hard cold unyielding floor on her back adding to the pain of his angry thrusts. When he was finished, he got off her, pulled up his pants then spit in her face.

"Whore" he screamed at her. "You are lousy in bed anyway. I don't know why I wasted my time on you. I should have let all of those other guys help themselves that night. You might have learned that I am the one in control here, and from now on you will do what I say." Then he walked out. Faith heard him stumble down the stairs then out the apartment door.

She laid thereon the floor in disbelief, not understanding what had taken place. Painfully, using the edge of the tub to pull herself up, she got to her feet gathering her torn stained clothes around her.

She had never felt so used or degraded in her life. Her head and neck were sore from being dragged around. Running her hand through her hair, large clumps torn out by the roots came away in her fingers. Her body was a mass of welts and bruises. Looking in the mirror she saw a bruise on her cheek, her top lip was bleeding and there were finger prints on her throat. She filled the tub with hot water wincing as she sat down. Then she cried.

"What did I do to deserve this?" she asked herself. "What did I say? Why? I don't understand any of this."

Wrapping herself in a towel she went into the spare room, locked the door, climbed into bed and cried until she fell into an exhausted sleep.

SIX

The next morning she could barely crawl out of bed, every part of her hurt, even inside where he had rammed himself into her. Opening the bedroom door she looked to see if Lance had come home but there was no sign of him. Spurred into action she dressed quickly in a long sleeved black pantsuit and a turtle neck sweater, taking extra care with her makeup to cover the bruise on her cheek. As she painfully combed her hair, more clumps fell into the bathroom sink. Frantically she stuffed several changes of clothes into an overnight bag.

"I have to get out of here before he comes back," she muttered to herself. "I can't live like this anymore. I know I have to make some decisions, but I don't know where to go or what to do. How did I ever let things get to this point?"

First she called a taxi, then picked up her coat, purse and bag and walked to the elevator. She hid in the shadows of the lobby until the taxi pulled up to the front door. The only place she could go to that would provide her any safety was the office.

She waved at Andrew as she walked in.

"Early aren't you Faith?"

"I've got lots to do today."

Arriving at the sixteenth floor she peered down the hallways before going into her office. She didn't want anyone to see her. She needed peace and quiet to think, to make some decisions. "Should I go home? No, my dad will throw this experience up at me for the rest of my life. Maybe I should move back in with Cassandra and find a new job away from here." In the end, she was just as undecided as she had been before.

The day was hectic. Cassandra was ill and had taken the day off. "So much for that idea" Faith thought.

When the day ended she still hadn't decided what to do. The one thing she knew for certain was that she wasn't going back to the apartment. She had already decided to stay at the office overnight.

At five, she left the building with the rest of the staff. She wandered down the street to a small cafe and tried to eat a roast beef sandwich with fries, but the food stuck in her throat. She left most of her meal on her plate. She was hungry, and hadn't eaten for more than twenty four hours but her jaw hurt too much to chew.

Faith stayed at the café until it closed at seven then walked slowly back to the office. Realizing Andrew was gone for the evening, she swiped her card in the side door and again in the elevator. Thankfully no one was working late tonight. For the first time in a long time she felt safe.

Going into the staff lounge, she laid down on one of the sofas and immediately fell asleep. She vaguely heard the cleaning staff chattering back and forth to each other as they cleaned the offices. Whoever cleaned the staff room must have done so very quietly because she hadn't heard a thing.

Once again she woke up stiff and sore. The pain was worse than the day before and brought tears to her eyes.

"Today," she told herself, "I have to make some kind of decision, but right now I don't feel capable of doing anything."

She went to her office, took some clean clothes from her overnight bag then went into the Ladies room. She had a shower, noticing that the bruises on her body were turning yellow and green. She quickly dressed and went back to her office and not a moment too soon. She heard the elevator door open and saw Mrs. Heatley get off and walk directly into her own office.

Briefly Faith thought about going to her, telling her what had taken place, but decided against it. There was no use getting somebody else involved in her problems.

She kept her office door closed until she heard some of the other staff arrive. Venturing into the staff lounge she poured herself a cup of coffee and took a bottle of juice from the fridge.

"You're here early this morning Faith." Mrs. Heatley remarked as she walked into the lounge.

"Couldn't sleep, so I decided to come in and finish the research I was working on yesterday."

"Faith I've noticed that you are making a real effort to get your life and work back on track. I am proud of you."

Tears filled Faith's eyes. Those were the first kind words she had heard in a long time.

"I am trying, "she replied to Mrs. Heatley. To herself she added "if you only knew the truth."

"How did you get that bruise on your cheek? Does it hurt?" inquired Mrs. Heatley.

"I tripped over a shoe and smashed my face against the edge of the coffee table. I always was a little clumsy," Faith explained, putting her hand up to the bruise on her face. Mrs. Heatley looked at her strangely then walked away. Why was Faith lying to her?

Just after three in the afternoon there was a knock on her door. Without looking up from her computer she answered, "come in."

It was Lance, his arms filled with the red roses.

Cowering behind her desk she glared at him. "Get away from me. Don't you dare come any closer or I will call Security, "she said, picking up the phone."

"Wait Faith please," he begged. "I'm sorry. I don't know what came over me."

"Get out!"

"Please listen to me. I didn't mean to hurt you. It's as if I blacked out and didn't know what I was doing. I'll quit drinking. I'll quit the drugs. No more women. We will get married just like you want. Please forgive me? I am so sorry."

Faith looked at him. His eyes were red, his face puffy. Part of her wanted to get away from him and put an end to this relationship. The other part felt sorry for him. Now she had the perfect excuse, if she chose to use it, to leave and start over.

"I was worried when you didn't come home last night" he continued. "When I saw your bloody clothes on the bathroom floor I realized what I had done to you, and how much I need you in my life. Will you come back to me? Can you ever forgive me for hurting you so?"

"Oh yes Lance I can. I love you and I need you too." She came out from behind her desk and took him into her arms. They stood there for a long time holding each other before they left for home together.

SEVEN

Faith had to give Lance credit, he was trying. Most evenings he stayed home with her. When he had to work late he called from the office to say when he was leaving and came directly home. He stopped drinking. She held his head, fed him and cleaned up behind him as he went through withdrawal from the drugs. All the while she continued to hope their relationship stood a chance.

Two months later Faith found herself retching into the toilet. Again! The first time she blamed what she had eaten the night before, then she blamed stress or maybe she had picked up a touch of the stomach flu. This morning was the worst ever. Her senses began reeling when she realized she might be pregnant.

"Oh God no, not this, not now," she moaned." We are getting along so well."

On her lunch hour she purchased a pregnancy test. Racing home after work she performed the test. She already knew the truth, but needed to see the confirmation. The result was positive just as she knew it would be.

Folding her arms across the closed lid of the toilet she put head on top of them crying the deep desperate sobs of a trapped animal. What was she going to do? Worse yet, how would Lance react? A part of her was happy they would be bringing a new life into this world together. The other part knew that a bad situation had suddenly become worse.

When her tears stopped, she realized that this child was probably the result of that terrifying night he had raped her or shortly after. There was no doubt in her mind she was going to keep this baby. She also decided that for the time being, she wasn't going to tell Lance, she would wait until the time was right. She wondered if there was even the faintest possibility that he would be happy. Could a new life waiting to be born cement them together forever?

One night, laying on the bed, basking in the afterglow of making love, Lance ran his finger across her breasts and down her stomach. "Seems to me you are getting a little pudgy around the middle and your breasts feel fuller. It's kind of nice. I like it."

Taking his hand in hers, then placing them both flat on her stomach "Not weight, our baby. I am three months pregnant. You are going to be a father."

At first he didn't say or do anything then he slowly lifted his hand from her stomach, looked her in the eyes and said "get rid of it! Tomorrow!" Then he rolled over and turned his naked back to her.

Faith didn't know what to think. In her mind she had been hoping for a different reaction. She had convinced herself that he would be pleased, and they would begin making wedding plans. She already had the details planned out.

"Lance?"

"Leave me alone. We'll talk in the morning."

Faith admonished herself. "This isn't going the way I planned. Maybe I should have waited for a while yet, until our life was on a more even keel, but I am beginning to show. He would have noticed sooner or later."

When she got up in the morning he was gone. She was relieved her secret was out in the open, and that she had finally told him. Given time to adjust, she was sure he would come around.

The next evening, on her way home from work she picked up two steaks, the trimmings for a Greek salad, a loaf of garlic bread and a bottle of low alcohol wine for a celebration supper. Now they would have to get married. Her dad would be disappointed, but once the baby came he would change his mind. Her mother would be absolutely delighted. If she could keep Lance sober he would be an excellent father.

When he came through the door, an hour late for supper, she saw he had been drinking. Her heart sank. Kissing him lightly on the cheek she helped him off with his jacket and led him to the table.

"Supper is ready," she said, pouring him a glass of wine and setting his plate in front of him. She served the steaks on a platter and placed the Greek salad she had made in the middle of the table.

He took three bites then threw his knife across the table. "Where did you buy this crap? My steak is so tough I can barely cut through it with my knife. Can't you do anything right?"

"Here take mine, it's nice and tender and I'm not that hungry anyway. Can I make you something else?" she said taking the steak off his plate and replacing it with hers

He looked at her with steely eyes, "You are going tomorrow to get rid of that kid. I have an appointment set up with a friend of mine who looks after mistakes like these.

"Is that what this is all about?" she fired back. "You tell me that I do everything wrong then think that gives you authority to make my decisions for me. Guess again Lance Palmer, I make my own decisions from now on. I am not having an abortion. I am going to keep this baby and raise him or her on my own. If you don't want to be a part of its life that's fine with me, I'm not getting rid of it just because you think I should."

He grabbed her by the wrist. "You listen to me; you will do what I tell you. For all I know this is some cheap trick to force me into marrying you. Guess what? It isn't going to work. There is no way I am going to spend the rest of my life paying for some brat that may not even be mine."

Faith recoiled as if he had slapped her. "Oh, it's yours alright. Does the fact that you say you don't remember raping me mean it can't be yours? Do you think I made the whole thing up? I am not having an abortion. I am staying here until the baby comes and you will pay support for the rest of your life. Now let go of me or I will call the police."

EIGHT

Faith finished typing the last of a brief she had been working on for one of the partners. Ten more minutes and she would be able to go home. Her feet were swollen, the baby was kicking her in the bladder and her head hurt from staring at the computer screen all afternoon. There was a soft knock on the door and Carole Adams from Accounting poked her head in.

"Are you busy Faith? I need someone to talk to."

"No, I'm finished. What a crazy day this has been. I'm leaving in ten minutes but I will always find time for you. What's up?"

"I need your advice. The Jasper family was in today and they raised hell. I thought Mr. Amos and Mrs. Heatley were both going to have a heart attack.

A year or so ago Mr. Jasper asked us to handle the sale of his house, for which he received two hundred thousand dollars. Shortly after he signed the sales agreement, but before the money was released, he got sick and ended up in the hospital. His money has been in a trust account ever since," she explained.

"He died last week. This morning his daughter came in asking us to handle his estate. She had done her homework, bringing in all of his papers including our receipt for the two hundred thousand dollars," she added.

"In order to get things started, John Walters did the intake. He called me to confirm we had money in trust for Mr. Jasper and how much there was. There was one hundred and fifty thousand dollars left in the account and five withdrawals of ten thousand each over a period of time. I reported this to John and Mr. Jasper's daughter lost it. She claimed her father had never touched the money. They went through the bills and she was right, he was in the hospital at the time all five withdrawals were made. John called in Mrs. Heatley who in turn called in Mr. Amos. Fifty thousand dollars was missing and nobody had any idea where it went or what it could have been used for.

Faith, what if they think I took the money? I have signing authority over all of the trust accounts and it's my responsibility to make sure there are no problems. You know I take my job very seriously."

"I know you do. Who was the initial lawyer on the house sale? Go back to him for verification."

"Faith" Carole said quietly, "it was Lance."

Instantly she sprang to his defense, "I'm sure he wouldn't take money from his clients' accounts Carole. He knows better than that."

"Wait, there is more. After everybody left and things settled down, I checked a couple more accounts. Every single trust account listed under Lance's name is short. The more money initially put into the account, the more was missing. In each case there is a series of withdrawals, all for the same amount, ten thousand dollars. When I looked at the time frames, all of this started shortly after Lance was moved into head office. Before then, there had been no problems."

Faith looked at her dumbfounded, "Carole, don't tell anybody about this. You can't accuse him without proof. We will go through the accounts together and document what we can, then go to the police. To say anything now will tip off whoever is actually committing the thefts."

"But you and Lance...."

Faith replied bitterly, "I owe him nothing. Once the baby comes I am leaving. Don't tell anyone that either. Until then, I have to keep working so I can put away enough money to manage without a cent from him. Our romance was over a long time ago."

A few days later Carole stopped Faith in the hallway. "Mr. Amos made Lance meet with the Jasper family and explain about the money. He claimed Mr. Jasper had encouraged him to take some of the money and invest it in the stock market - said Mr. Jasper had a hot tip he wanted to follow up on. Of course the market is down now and that is how much was lost before Lance stopped investing for him."

"He is lying. We never invest client's funds. We always put them in a high interest savings account and leave them there."

"I know" said Carole, scurrying away. Faith looked up to see Lance watching them from the other end of the hallway. She wanted to ask Carole what Mr. Jasper's daughter had said about that information.

"What was going on between you and Carole? She left like a scared rabbit." he quizzed her later.

"Nothing much, Carole was upset with her boyfriend and was telling me about his latest prank. Those two always seem to be having problems," she lied.

Faith stayed after work for the rest of the week checking the trust accounts of Lance's clients. She worked as quickly as she could, and if she thought there was a discrepancy, she photocopied the documents then added them to her ever growing file. At the end of each evening she locked the file in the back of one of her desk drawers.

During the next two weeks she took time to go through each document and scan it into her lap top. When she was finished, she realized that the sum of over one hundred thousand dollars had been withdrawn over twelve months. She then transferred all the information from her lap top onto a flash drive, and then taped it to the top shelf in her closet. She filed the paper copies in Carole's office in the back of one the least used filing cabinets. Then she went home to confront Lance.

The sound of his key turning in the lock woke her up. Her baby was due in four weeks and the additional bulk made her feel uncomfortable and tired most of the time. She had fallen asleep while waiting for him to come home.

"You still up?" Lance said. "How come?"

"Something came up at work I need to talk to you about."

"Not tonight. I'm tired. Whatever is on your little mind can wait until tomorrow. I am going to bed." Faith failed to notice the slight slurring of his words.

"No Lance it can't." she replied, standing up and putting her hands on her hips. "I know what you are doing."

"What do you mean know what I am doing? You are always imagining things. You tell me what you think is going on, and then we will both know what you are talking about."

"Lance I know about the money you are stealing from your client's accounts. You have got to stop and put that money back right away before somebody figures out who it is. You could go to jail."

"What in the hell are you talking about? What money? Stop what?"

"The money missing from your clients trust accounts. I know that you have been stealing from them and how much you have taken."

Instead of denying her accusation, he looked at her and ranted "So now you are going to play Miss Innocent on me. Did you really think I can afford this life style on a Lawyer's salary? You drank a lot of that money and snorted it up your nose yourself."

"You can't blame any of this on me. I had no idea, "retorted Faith.

"So now that you have this information what do you think you're going to do? Turn me in? Without proof you can't do a damn thing, it will be your word against mine."

"I have proof."

He slapped her across the face knocking her backward over the arm of the sofa. "You are not going to tell anyone. Do you hear me?"

Suddenly Faith was tired of being bullied and pushed around by him. Getting back onto her feet she threatened him "You touch me again and I will make sure the whole world knows that you are a thief, an alcoholic and a drug addict. I will smear your name all over this town. This fancy apartment and your good life will be over. You know something, you are no better than the scum you hang out with."

She didn't see the punch coming. Lance slammed his fist into her stomach knocking the wind out of her. She fell to the floor. He was upon her, straddling her shoulders slapping her face from one side to the other, her head bouncing off the floor.

"You say one word about this and I will kill you." he hissed into her face. She struggled to get out from under him but he was too heavy.

"Get off me. I can't breathe" she begged. "I won't tell anybody. I promise."

He got up on his feet. "Tomorrow you take your fat pregnant belly and get the hell out of my life. I can't even stand to look at you."

Then, without warning, he drew back his foot and kicked her in the stomach as hard as he could. She fainted from the pain.

Minutes later, when she came to she was alone, still lying on the floor. Curling up into a ball she cried. Later when she tried to stand up excruciating pain in her back forced her back down. A fresh wave of pain doubled her over, and when she looked down her legs were covered with blood and fluid. Crawling into the kitchen, she pulled the portable phone off the cupboard and dialed 9-1-1.

"What is your emergency?" a voice said.

"My baby is coming. Please help me."

"Where are you located, in what apartment?" The dispatch computer brought up the name and address of her building but not the individual apartments.

"Apartment twenty one ten."

"Help is on its way. Is your apartment door unlocked?"

"No, but I'll do that. Please hurry."

Faith pulled herself to her feet using the cupboard to steady herself. The last thing she remembered was unlocking and opening the apartment door. When the paramedics arrived, they found her laying half in and half out of the doorway

Drifting in and out of consciousness she was vaguely aware of what was happening around her. There were voices. She heard the siren of the ambulance, saw the flashing lights overhead as she was rushed down the hospital corridor; felt something put over her face, then darkness.

Many hours later she opened her eyes. "Oh God I hurt, "she moaned. Her first instinct was to put her hands on her stomach to make sure the baby was OK but her stomach was flat. The baby was gone. She began screaming. A nurse and intern ran into her room.

"Miss Benson, what's the matter?"

"My baby, the blood…. My baby is dead isn't it? He killed my baby. Please tell me."

"Miss Benson, everything is alright." The nurse reassured her. "Your baby is not dead; he is in the Neonatal Intensive Care Unit. You have a beautiful four pound baby boy who has lots of hair the same color as yours. He has had a pretty rough start for someone so small so we are going to keep him in there for a few days."

"Can I see him? I have to see him for myself" she cried out hysterically.

"Miss Benson, I assure you he is fine. You need to get some rest. Both of you are lucky to be alive after what you went through. I'll check with your doctor. If he says you can get out of bed I will take you to see him after lunch."

"What happened? I don't remember very much," she replied much calmer.

"The paramedics found you have in and half out of your apartment door. You were hemorrhaging and unconscious. When you arrived here, it was touch and go for a while but you made it through. Apparently someone broke into your apartment and beat you up. Your boyfriend arrived home the same time as the paramedics got there. When you arrived here we had to do an emergency caesarean to save your baby and stop the bleeding. You are both going to be fine. You will have other babies, but they will have to be by caesarean section also, Rest now and I will be back for you soon."

After the nurse left, Faith lay there smiling to herself, a little boy. She had already decided that, if her baby was a boy, she would call him Josh.

She awoke when she heard someone enter her room. Opening her eyes she saw Lance standing there with a big bouquet of red roses and a blue teddy bear in his arms. He tried to kiss her on the cheek.

"What do you want?" she snapped. "Get out of here."

"I came to see our baby. I'm sorry Faith; I never meant to hurt you or our son. Please forgive me. I never realized how important you were in my life until I nearly lost you."

She looked at him coldly and said "Don't you ever touch me again."

Before Lance could retaliate the nurse came in with a wheel chair. Lance carefully lifted her out of bed, and placed her in the chair as if she were a china doll. Together they went down the hallway to the Neonatal Intensive Care Unit. Inside, the nurse wheeled her to an isolette in the back corner which contained the most beautiful, smallest baby Faith had ever seen.

"Do you want to hold him?" the nurse asked. She lifted the side of the isolette and took out the tiny baby, placing him in Faith's arms. She looked him over; ten fingers and ten toes. As she ran her hand over his face his tiny hand reached up and latched onto one of her fingers.

Faith was astonished at the out pouring of love she felt while holding her baby. She glanced at Lance, hoping he would feel the same but he was looking the other way with a very bored look on his face.

Holding the tiny baby in her arms she whispered, "You are mine and I will never let you go. I promise you will have a better life than I have."

"Miss Benson, we have to put him back now. He is doing great so far, and if he remains stable over the next twenty four hours, we will move him to the nursery. We will keep him there except for feedings. We want to make sure that you don't have any complications from your surgery and get some rest before we move him into your room."

Faith handed the baby back to her and watched as he was returned to his cocoon of warmth. "I am going to call him Josh." She was very much aware that Lance hadn't said a word since they had left her room.

Upon returning to her room the nurse helped her back into bed. Lance was standing in the doorway his face expressionless. He didn't say a word nor offer to help Faith in any way.

"I've got to go," he said and was gone.

"Miss Benson, the police are here and want to talk to you about what took place last night. Are you up to seeing them?'

'Not right now. Please ask them to come back later. I'm very tired."

Once she was alone Faith tried to think about what she needed to do. Mentally she made a list. Before she left the hospital she would have to find a place to live, go on maternity leave and somehow get away from Lance. With her savings and maternity leave benefits she would be OK for a while. Then she slept.

Several hours later she heard a male voice, "Miss Benson, can we talk now?"

Faith opened her eyes to see a man and a woman standing beside her bed.

"My name is Detective Don Sharp and this is my partner Detective Sandy Rowan, We want to ask you a few questions about last night. Do you feel up to answering them?"

"Yes, let's get this over with," she replied wearily.

"Did you see the face of who did this to you?"

"No, he wore a black mask."

"Do you have any idea how he got into your apartment."

"I'm not sure. I must not have closed the door securely when I got home. I was tired."

"What did he want?"

"Money. I gave him all I had in my purse but he wanted more. When I didn't have any more to give him he started hitting me."

Faith knew she was lying but she had no choice. Everything she owned was in Lance's apartment including her purse. She had already decided that, until she was stronger and Josh was bigger, she was going to stay where she was. She was trapped in this terrible situation and needed time to find a way out. She also realized now that she had confronted Lance about the money, he was dangerous. If she willingly went back to his apartment he wouldn't be suspicious of anything she did.

The next morning Cassandra arrived with her arms filled with gifts and flowers. The office staff had pooled their money and bought her a car seat.

"Hey honey, how are you doing? I come bearing gifts." Cassandra said lightly as she came through the door.

Faith looked at her, smiled weakly, and then began to cry. Instantly Cassandra was beside her bed and took her hand.

"Oh my Lord, look at you. Whoever did this did a real number on you. Don't try and tell me an intruder did this. I know you are more careful than that. Did Lance do this to you?"

Seeing Faith's stricken face Cassandra stopped mid-sentence. "He did, didn't he?"

Faith nodded yes.

"That S O B, wait until I get my hands on him."

"Cassandra you can't tell anybody. Nobody must know."

"Why not? Personally, I don't think much of a man who beats up a woman who is eight months pregnant. He has no right....."

Faith stopped her mid-sentence. "Please Cassandra; going after him will only make things worse. I have to go back to his place until I am stronger. I don't know what else to do. As soon as I am able, I am going to find another job and leave him."

"That is the stupidest thing I've ever heard you say. He'll do this to you again."

"No, he won't. I know things about him that he doesn't want made public. If he ever hits me again I have the power to get him thrown in jail."

"You can't be serious. What's to stop him from doing this any time he feels like punching somebody around?"

"Cassandra, I have no place to go. After all he is Josh's father"

"That jerk doesn't deserve to have either one of you."

"Please don't make a fuss. I have a plan. I know what I am doing, probably for the first time in months."

Cassandra tried to change Faith's mind but she couldn't. Faith was adamant.

As she was leaving, Cassandra looked at her and said sincerely, "you promise me that if you ever need anything, you will call me. If he goes after you again he will have me to deal with."

Three days later she and little Josh were discharged. Lance put on quite a show acting like the warm caring boyfriend who couldn't wait to get his little family home. Faith knew the whole scene was a farce being acted out for the benefit of the nurses. Knowing that she currently had no other options she went along with his little charade

NINE

Faith stayed inside the apartment recuperating and getting to know her baby. Mothering came naturally to her. Lance rarely came home, and when he did he was either drunk or high. At night she locked herself into Josh's room. More than once he had awakened her by pounding on the door, calling her names, demanding his right to have sex with her. He screamed at her saying that he owned her and it was time for her to stop paying so much attention to the kid and start looking after his needs. Other times he ranted and raved that he was going to kill the two of them, throw their bodies into the river and be rid of them once and for all.

These times were the worst. She started keeping a knife in her room and would push it into the door jamb to make it harder for him if he tried to force door open. Other times she would take Josh from his crib and hide behind the bed until he left. She lived in constant terror, never knowing if this was the time he would beat down the door and follow through on his threats.

Faith was relieved that Mrs. Heatley had arranged for her to work from home on a contract basis. Now she had her own money coming in, even though it was considerably less than before.

"Little Josh" she said one day, "it's time for me to show you off." Rather than e-mailing her report she decided to go the office and deliver it by hand. She was getting tired of being cooped up and alone.

When she exited the elevator Evelyn saw her first. By the time Faith had taken the baby out of his lounge chair Evelyn had snatched him from her hands. She left Faith standing in the hallway as she paraded the baby from one office to the other.

"Faith" Mrs. Heatley called out to her "how good to see you again. Come into my office for a minute?" Closing the door she looked at Faith and asked bluntly "how are you doing?"

With tears welling in her eyes Faith answered, "not very well."

"Do you want to talk?"

"No" Faith replied. "I got myself into this mess I have to get myself out."

Mrs. Heatley reached over and took one of her a business cards from the acrylic holder on her desk and wrote a number on the front. "This is my home number. Promise me you will call if you need help."

Taking the card Faith replied gratefully, "thank you for being here for me Mrs. Heatley. I promise to call if I need to."

"If you wish, you may call me Elizabeth from now on. Faith, have you thought of going home to your parents? We will give you a leave of absence for a few months and you can continue working for us on a contract basis while you are there. I think being with your parents would be good for you right now."

"I can't go home. My parents don't know about Lance or Josh. I haven't spoken to them for over a year."

Mrs. Heatley looked at her pointedly and said," maybe you need to give them a call."

Faith heard Josh crying in the hallway and jumped to her feet. "He is probably hungry. I had better go relieve Evelyn so she can get back to work. Elizabeth, Mrs. Heatley, I will think about what you said. No promises though."

Faith took the baby from Evelyn's arms, gathered her belongings, and went to the staff lounge. As he nursed she looked around. "It would be hard to leave this place. I would miss working here."

She was burping him when Carole came into the room, looking around furtively to make sure they were alone. She sat down beside Faith on the sofa.

"Faith, I thought you might like to know that Mrs. Amos had a team of forensic auditors come in. They found that there is more than one hundred fifty thousand dollars missing from all of the trust accounts."

"Do they know who is responsible yet?"

"If they do, they aren't saying. Mr. Amos and Mr. Northrup arranged to put all of the missing money back but now the firm is in jeopardy of closing. They have already closed the East side office and let some of the staff here go. They handed Lance the Winsome case. If he can win that one, the firm has a chance of surviving."

Faith felt sick to her stomach. She was under the impression Lance had stopped stealing when she confronted him. Apparently, the loss was even more than she had been able to trace.

Lance came home early for supper that evening and stayed with her and Josh. For once he was sober. Watching him hold their son renewed Faith's hope that one day they might still become a real family.

"I heard you two were at the office today."

"Yes. I was tired of sitting in this apartment all the time so I decided to deliver the papers I was working on for Mrs. Heatley. Besides, I thought it was time to show off our beautiful son."

"I saw you in the staff lounge talking to Carole."

"That was nothing." she reassured him. "She was upset because auditors had come in and gone through her work."

As soon as Faith said those words she knew she had made a mistake

"Auditors, what did they want?"

Trying to cover up she explained, "It is a usual practice. They come in once a year, maybe the firm is getting ready to do its year end."

Then she stopped herself. What was the point in coddling him any further? "Actually she told me there are thousands of dollars more missing than they originally thought. I begged you to stop taking money from those accounts a long time ago. If you get caught you will end up in jail. I can't even begin to imagine why you needed so much."

"Did you say anything about me?"

"No, I wouldn't do that."

His next words chilled her to the bone. "If you ever say one word to anybody I will take that kid away from you and put him up for adoption."

Faith laid her sleeping baby on the sofa, rose to her feet and looked at him. "I have had enough of your threats. I am taking Josh and leaving right now." she said turning to pick up her son.

He grabbed her arm, twisting it behind her back. "You're not going any place." he hissed in her face, "You will stay away from the office from now on and you will talk to no one from there. I won't hesitate for a minute to get rid of that kid if you disobey me."

"Lance let go, you are hurting me. I have no intention of telling anybody your dirty little secret. I haven't yet and I won't. I promise."

"Good "he said dropping her arm "you and that damn kid are nothing but trouble.

TEN

True to her word Faith stayed away from the office. Lance continued to become more and more paranoid. Each day he went through her e-mails and checked the call display on the phone. Mrs. Heatley had called several times, and after each call Lance had given her the third degree insisting upon being told what the calls were about. Thankfully they were work related. He had taken her bank and credit cards from her purse changed the passwords and refused to tell her what the new ones were. This left her with no way to access her accounts. If she needed money she had to ask him for the amount she thought she would need, and then bring home receipts accounting for every penny she had spent. She even had to give him the change to the exact penny. He also started calling all hours of the day, and if she didn't answer he demanded a full explanation of where she had been. She had become a prisoner in her home.

Then, to her surprise one evening he said "you and the brat are coming to Devil's Bay with me tomorrow for the corporate retreat. Be ready by ten."

"I would rather not go" she replied, "Josh and I will stay here. You go ahead."

"Do you really think I am going to leave you here alone? I said you are coming and that's final! Everyone is to bring their family and I don't want to have to spend the entire weekend explaining why you didn't come with me. Besides, I don't trust you. You are liable to take my kid and run."

"Oh, so now he's your kid is he?" she taunted him.

"Shut up Faith. I said you are coming and that's final."

Devil's Bay, a world class resort, was located across the bay on Devils Island. Located on a peninsula, the main buildings were bordered on two sides by the Pacific Ocean. There was a golf course and sandy beaches edged with lush green lawns and flowering shrubs.

Each year the corporate office rented the entire resort for three days. It was a gesture for the wives and children, in appreciation for the long business hours that the men were away from their families. The associates and partners spent each morning in strategy sessions. In the afternoons they were free to be with their families or play in the daily golf tournaments. On the Saturday evening there was a steak barbecue and an informal awards and recognition night. Because of the two big law suits he had won during the year, Lance was counting upon being offered a full partnership. He had won the Winsome case thus protecting the integrity and financial status of the firm.

Their four hour trip was made in strained silence, neither of them speaking to the other. Josh slept all of the way.

Upon arrival Faith began to relax. The sound of the sea, the warm sand and the fresh ocean breeze were healing for her. Lance was attentive, showing off his son like every other doting father. Faith felt content for the first time in months. This was the Lance she had fallen in love with. This was the man he should be, not the terrible monster hidden behind the mask he wore.

She spent much of her time alone with Josh, deliberately choosing to stay away from the groups of other young wives. Although she yearned to be part of their chattering laughing group, she reminded herself it was safer this way. She didn't want to spend her time in this idyllic place trying to explain to Lance who she had talked to and what they had talked about.

She and Josh watched the other children playing in the sand running away from the incoming waves. Sometimes she took him to the water's edge to let him feel the sand and water on his feet. He laughed when the water tickled his toes. Other times she carried him on her back as she walked along the beach, telling him of the wonderful things they were going to do and the marvelous places they were going to see. She shared her dream of her and Lance getting married and having a house in suburbia with a white picket fence. Josh had no idea what she was talking about but appeared to be listening and understanding as she droned on.

Josh was asleep in his stroller. Faith was sitting on a park bench watching the rise and fall of the ocean feeling more and more desperate. These few days of rest and relaxation helped her realize she had to get away from Lance. Their situation would continue to deteriorate until something drastic happened. Even if he wanted to get married she would refuse. She was now painfully aware that getting mixed up with Lance had been the biggest mistake of her life. She wished she had listened to Cassandra and taken her advice.

Startling Faith out of her day dream Elizabeth Heatley asked "May I join you?"

"Of course, I love sitting here watching the waves and Josh is having such a good sleep I don't want to disturb him. He is teething and a little fussy at times."

Elizabeth Heatley had been watching Faith since her arrival noticing that she stayed to herself and kept her baby close. The once vivacious young girl was now haggard looking and sad. There were dark circles under her eyes and she was extremely thin. She had also noticed how possessive Lance was of her and how Faith unconsciously flinched and pulled away each time he touched her. Something was terribly wrong.

"I've missed you at the office. You haven't come around for a while but I must say your reports are their usual excellent quality."

"Thank you "Faith said sadly, "I miss everyone there too."

"Faith, I know this is none of my business but is everything OK between you and Lance. Are you having problems?"

Faith didn't answer for a long time, then she said "Mrs. Heatley, Elizabeth, I am in trouble and don't know what to do."

"You can tell me if you wish Faith. You know I will keep what you say in strictest confidence. When I saw you sitting here, I sensed you needed a friend."

Once unleashed, a torrent of brutally honest words spewed from Faith's mouth. Elizabeth listened as Faith told her about giving Lance her virginity, the booze and drug filled nights, how he had beat, and then raped her on the bath room floor. She told her how he had kicked her the night Josh was born, nearly killing both of them. She explained that she wanted to get away from him but stayed because he was threatening her. The only information she kept to herself was the story of the missing money. She wanted to say something, but that was the only weapon she had that would help her keep Josh.

79

When finished she said sadly. "I have been such a fool. I can't understand how I let him control me, and allowed him to drag me into the gutter with him. I am so ashamed. Sometimes I wish I had died that terrible night. I guess this is what my dad meant when he used to say, "You made your bed now lie in it."

Elizabeth Heatley knew there had been problems between the two of them but this story of repeated abuse shocked her. She could see that Lance Palmer was destroying this young girl, using her for his own sexual and personal gratification. She was acutely aware of the fact that Faith had been over protected at home and unprepared for living in the city. In a way she felt responsible. She had hired her based upon her excellent qualifications; never once thinking about the girl herself and how overwhelming it must have been to leave her small town.

What saddened her most was to learn that the actions of such a brilliant young lawyer made him a liability to the firm." What a waste," she told herself.

After Faith had finished speaking Elizabeth said to her "I can't tell you what to do but my advice is to take Josh and go home. Your parents will forgive you. How could they not when you have such a beautiful baby?"

"No, my dad will never forgive me. Every time he gets drunk he will rant and rave about how he was right. In some ways he is no different than Lance except that he doesn't lash out with his fists. He lets his tongue do all the work."

"Faith I am going to ask you a tough question. If you had no other choice would you be willing to leave Josh with Lance in order to save yourself? This may come to that one day."

"I don't know. I don't think I can trust Lance not to put him up for adoption or take out his temper on him. I'm afraid he will hurt Josh to get back at me. My little boy is the only thing that keeps me going day after day."

"Personally, I think that if you left, Lance would play the "Poor me Faith walked out leaving me with this kid to look after" card. He will make sure we all know that now he is paying for a housekeeper to look after him. He will make a big deal of everything. He will put you down; probably call you every name he can think of, but he will keep Josh safe. Lance needs him to get you back."

"Do you really think that's what he would do?"

"Lance loves attention, and with all of us feeling sorry for him, he will be in his glory. Think about what I have said and see if any of this conversation offers you any new or more options. I can't tell you what to do, that's your decision, but I can promise to do what I can to support you."

Lance was in a good mood when she returned to their suite. He played with Josh and teased her about her sunburned nose. Secretly Faith had been hoping that, after this weekend, their relationship would change for the better. She wanted him to feel like that he could trust her again. She hoped he would see that she had every opportunity to tell someone about him stealing the money and had said nothing.

At the recognition barbecue Faith was surprised to receive a plaque for excellence and one thousand dollars in cash. Lance didn't receive the partnership offer he was expecting. Although he was livid, he did a good job of covering up his feelings.

He didn't come back to their suite that night. At noon the next day he showed up hung over, in a foul mood wanting to leave. Quickly she packed. She didn't want to go back to the city but she couldn't see any other way out of this mess. Elizabeth, with all of her good intentions didn't understand how vicious he could be.

As soon as she got into the car he started picking at her. "This is your fault" he screamed at her, "having that brat made me look bad in the eyes of the company. You should have had that abortion like I wanted you to, but no, you had to have the baby. You are the reason I didn't get that partnership offer. For all I know you were blabbing everything to that Mrs. Heatley and the two of you conspired to put a stop to my promotion. I saw the two of you sitting by the beach talking. You never learn do you?"

"Lance, I didn't say anything to her. We were just talking about the office. I miss going to work every day. Besides, this is not my fault. I have no control over who is offered a full partnership that is up to Mr. Amos and Mr. Northrup. You know that."

"Shut up. When we get home I will show you whose fault it is."

Faith was terrified. When he was like this, he was unpredictable. She had no doubt in her mind that one day he would beat her until she was either crippled or dead.

The ferry ride back to the mainland took two hours giving Faith time to think. Was Mrs. Heatly right? Would Lance take good care of Josh if she left him behind? At some point she knew she had to trust somebody and listen to their advice. As the ferry was pulling into the dock she made a decision. She was going to take Josh and hide in the bathroom, then ask for help. This would be her one and only chance to get away from him.

An announcement came over the loud speaker "please return to your vehicles, we will be docking in five minutes."

This was her chance. "You go down to the car" she said "I have to go to the bathroom. I'll be right behind you." Picking up Josh she started to walk away.

"Leave him with me." he said, taking the baby out of her arms "I'll put him in his car seat. You had better hurry up; we will be able to drive off soon. Honestly I don't believe you, always leaving things to the last minute. You should have gone to the bathroom before it was time to get off the ferry.

"How could I do that? I didn't know I had to go until now. Once we are on the highway you know you won't stop."

In the bathroom Faith rested her elbows on the sink, cradling her head in her hands. She didn't know what to do. Then, taking a deep breath, she walked out of the room, back to Lance and their baby.

"I can't leave you with him Josh. I have to go back. I can live with whatever he puts me through because I have to protect you." she said out loud. "What will be, will be. I can't fight him anymore."

When she got back to their seats Josh and Lance were gone. Realizing they must have gone to the car she made her way downstairs to C level where the car was parked. The exit doors were open; the first cars on the other side were already driving off.

Lance's window was open. She could see his elbow resting on the window ledge and hear him talking someone on his cell phone. She heard him say "I don't know where that fat cow is. She had better get back here soon and look after this kid. I have to drive off in a minute. I have been in a deep freeze all weekend and need some of you hot loving.. Baby, you know what I mean, the kind only you can provide."

She turned and ran blindly back up the stairs. In a panic she ran back into the bathroom locking herself into one of the stalls. After hearing what he had said about her she couldn't go back with him.

Then a feeling of calm washed over her. She walked to the ticket booth and bought a bus ticket for the city. She walked down the ramp, mingling with the other departing passengers, and got on the bus. She could see Lance pulled off to the side, waiting for her, the four way flashers blinking on the car. He was pacing back and forth like cat stalking its prey. She found a seat on the right hand side of the bus then slumped down so he wouldn't see her from the road.

"Forgive me Josh" she pleaded. "This is the way things have to be for now. I promise I will come and get you. I promise. I will never leave you."

Lance was still pacing as the bus pulled away.

When the bus arrived in the city Faith got off and sat on a sidewalk bench sobbing uncontrollably. She had no idea of where to go or what to do. One man stopped to ask what was wrong but she couldn't tell him. Another couple walked by, and she heard one say to the other "she should be arrested. Drunks carrying on like that shouldn't be allowed to hang around public places."

She sat there until the sun went down then started walking. She walked without thinking where she was going, or about the danger that surrounded her. The bus depot was located in the seediest part of the city. Anything could happen. In fact, she was hoping someone would put her out of her misery. Life without Josh wouldn't be worth living.

Unsure how she got there, she realized she was standing in front of Cassandra's house. The living room light was still on. She rang the doorbell and waited. She didn't know what she would do if Cassandra turned her away.

After what seemed a long time, Cassandra opened the door. She took one look at Faith standing there, put her arms around her and led her inside. Faith was shivering, her teeth chattering violently. Cassandra led her to the couch and wrapped her in a blanket then went into the kitchen, returning with two cups of hot tea which she placed upon the coffee table in front of them. Gathering Faith into her arms Cassandra rocked her like a baby. Not a word had passed between them.

Soon the shivering stopped and Faith began to cry, deep heart wrenching sobs Cassandra cried with her. She had heard the rumors of Lances drinking, drug use and violent temper. She had seen him at the Pub flirting and leaving with a different woman every night. Some of them were so young she doubted they were of legal drinking age.

Eventually Faith began to calm down. "Right now, at this very moment I am safe," she reminded herself.

"Faith, whenever you are ready to talk, I'm here to listen." Cassandra said.

Faith sat there silently. Cassandra waited.

Finally Faith whispered very softly. "God forgive me, I left my baby with him. How I wish I had listened to you. I wish I had died instead of having to go through this."

The two girls sat quietly side by side. Faith's breathing became rhythmical and steady. Cassandra looked over and saw she was sleeping. She lifted Faith's head gently off her shoulder pushing her body in the opposite direction until she was lying down. Then she lifted her legs up on the sofa and rearranged the blanket. Wrapping herself in another blanket she turned on the T V and guarded her sleeping friend all night. The two cups of tea remained untouched on the table.

Several times Faith cried out, and then would settle again. Cassandra couldn't imagine what or how much her friend had suffered. To make the decision to leave Josh with Lance must have been pure hell, an act of desperation by a desperate woman. She promised herself she would see her friend through this ordeal no matter what she had to do, or how long it took. Faith didn't deserve this.

Cassandra, unsure of her next step, rummaged through Faith's purse looking for the phone number of her parents. Usually she would have thought twice about going into another woman's purse, but this was an emergency. She found nothing except Mrs. Heatley's business card with the hand written number on the front. At five thirty in the morning she phoned.

"Mrs. Heatley, this is Cassandra. I'm sorry to bother you this early in the morning. I won't be coming into work today. Faith showed up here several hours ago, alone and in terrible condition. I feel like I should stay with her. Emotionally she is a wreck. She must have walked a long way because her feet are blistered and bleeding."

"Do you have any idea what happened before she got there?"

"No. All she has told me so far is that she left the baby with Lance. "

"Will you call me later when you find out more? That poor child has been through more than any one person should have to bear. Cassandra, take all the time you need with her. Be strong because she needs a friend right now. Thank you for calling me. Keep in touch."

"I'll call you later when I know more about what has happened."

Three hours later Faith woke up with a start. Her head ached, and her feet were burning. Cassandra appeared with two mugs of steaming hot coffee.

"Honey, if you are going to keep me up all night, I have to know the reason why."

Once Faith began talking she couldn't stop. "Lance has virtually kept me a prisoner these past few months, reading my e-mails, changing the access codes to my bank accounts, and controlling my days by phoning at odd times. If I didn't answer his questions he threatened or lectured me. Other times he would use me as a human punching bag, always hitting me in places that didn't show any bruises."

"Why did you put up with that? Why didn't you leave?" Cassandra asked.

"He threatened to take Josh away and put him up for adoption. Everything was going good we were enjoying the weekend. I could see the Lance I love emerge from under the stress. I thought he would see how good the three of us were together, that we could make this work.

He saw Elizabeth and me sitting by the water talking and demanded that I tell him every word we said to each other. I was afraid to tell him because I knew how angry he would get. Opening up to her made me realize the only way to save Josh was to save myself first. As long as he has Josh he will think he has control over me and that I will have to do whatever he wants. I hope Mrs. Heatley knows what she was talking about. If not, I have walked away from the only person who matters in my life.

When he wasn't offered the full partnership he blamed me. Said I made him look bad in front of the corporate staff by having his baby." she added

"Of course" Cassandra snidely remarked "you got pregnant all by yourself, he had nothing to do with it. Doesn't he realize that his actions have consequences, that life is not all fun and games?"

Faith began crying again. "He had made arrangements to sell me to his friends for one evening and was charging them two hundred dollars each. They, including him, were going to use me to live out their sexual fantasies, like I was some piece of meat to be passed around. When I stood up to him he beat and raped me. I am sure Josh is the result of that night."

Cassandra was speechless. She knew that things hadn't been going well between them, but she was having difficulty comprehending the story her friend was telling her. How she must have suffered at his hand and told no one.

"So, he was the one who beat you so badly the night Josh was born. I thought so but wasn't sure. Why didn't you report him to the police?"

"Yes. He was the one. This time I was afraid to go back to the apartment. I could see he was barely controlling his anger and I knew what was coming. I couldn't let him beat me again, I don't think I would have survived. At the very last minute I decided not to get off the ferry. I tried to keep Josh with me, but Lance insisted upon taking him down to the car. Now I have to find a way to get him away from that monster," she sobbed hysterically.

"Faith, I don't understand, why did you would keep going back to him?"

"You saw what I had become. He made a point of telling me how lucky I was that he cared, no other man in this world who would want me after what I had done. I believed him. Cassandra, I loved him. What if he was right? At least when I was with him, I knew where I stood."

"Look honey, I am going to take a couple days off and stay with you. Try to get some rest."

Cassandra was deeply concerned for her friend. Something wasn't right. She was speaking in monotones, as if passing on a story she had heard. The only time she showed any real emotion was when she talked about Josh.

Faith slept most of the next two days. Cassandra was in contact with Mrs. Heatley several times a day. They were both beginning to wonder if they should take her to the hospital, maybe she needed more help than what they could give her.

True to form, Lance walked into the office on Monday morning carrying the crying baby. Handing him to Evelyn, he said "do something with this kid."

"Where's Faith?"

"She left me." he proclaimed loudly. "Just walked out, leaving me to look after this kid. I never should have got mixed up with her in the first place. I knew she was unstable and hooked on drugs, but I never thought she would walk out and leave him."

Evelyn stared at him. It took every ounce of self-control she had not to scratch his eyes out. "Why you arrogant so and so," she thought to herself, "good for her. Just who do you think you are fooling Lance Palmer?"

Evelyn took the crying child from him. His clothes were dirty, his diaper soggy. Lance handed her a blue and white diaper bag and Evelyn disappeared down the hall way.

In the bathroom she filled a sink with warm water, removed the dirty clothes and sat him in the sink. She bathed him, dressed him in the clean clothes she found in the diaper bag then went in search of something to feed him. She doubted that Lance had given him much to eat. She found some graham crackers in the cupboard and a container of yogurt in the fridge. After eating, he settled into her arms and went to sleep. She made a bed for him in one corner of the room using a cushion from a chair as a mattress and covered him with the blue fuzzy blanket she found in the diaper bag.

Lance was the center of attention. Everybody was curious and he was filling them in with quite a story. Evelyn felt sick as she heard him brazenly telling lies about Faith.

In the back ground Mrs. Heatley was working the phone. She phoned a former employee of hers, and after explaining the situation, talked her into working as a temporary housekeeper and nanny for Lance. She made arrangements for Josh to have a place in the building's day care. Lance could afford to pay and she wanted to be able to assure Faith that Josh was in good hands. Faith had trusted her, followed her suggestions, now it was her turn to step up just as she had promised

When her plans were complete she phoned Cassandra telling her what she had done. This was an imperfect solution at best, but all she could do on short notice. Lance had done exactly what she told Faith he would do. Little Josh was safe for now. She knew that, with a little persuasion, Lance would accept the life line she was about to offer him.

ELEVEN

Faith wasn't sure what Lance would do if he found her. She knew she was safe at Cassandra's for the time being because Lance had never taken her home. She stayed close to home, not going out in public unless she had to.

Cassandra kept her updated on what was going on at the office and any news concerning Lance and Josh. She was deeply concerned about Cassandra's welfare when she heard that Lance had been questioning her.

"Tell me what happened? "Faith inquired when an obviously shaken Cassandra came home from work.

"He cornered me in the coffee room and wanted to know where you were. I told him I thought you had gone back home, but he didn't believe me. He said that if I am talking to you that he needs to ask you some things about Josh."

"What did you say?"

"I told him that even if I did know, he was the last person I would tell."

"Oh, Cassandra, you need to be careful. He is a very dangerous man and will stop at nothing to get what he wants."

"Honey, you stop worrying about me and look after you. I can handle him," Cassandra assured her.

Lance continued playing the role of the wounded hero and calling her down to anyone who would listen. She also worried about her financial situation. She wouldn't let Cassandra support her and insisted on paying her own way, but the thousand dollars cash she had been awarded was quickly dwindling away. She dismissed the idea of going to her bank. If he was still watching her account that would alert him she was still in the city. Cassandra had spread the rumor that Faith had gone home to live with her parents.

Three blocks down her street was a family grocery store with a Help Wanted sign in the window. Faith had worked as a cashier at a movie store during the summer holidays to pay for college. She thought "maybe I have enough experience to qualify for this job". When she finally did apply the young couple was more than happy to hire her. She started the next day.

Faith was a hard worker and preferred to work the evening shift because that was when she missed Josh the most. She started at three in the afternoon and was usually home by ten. The pay was quite a bit less than she had been making, but this job gave her back the feeling of independence

One morning, in the staff lounge, Shelly Baker, one of the other Legal Assistants, was talking to Cassandra as they were pouring their morning coffee.

"Guess who I ran into last night, Faith Benson. She's working as a clerk at the Mi Lei grocery store not too far from my place."

"It couldn't have been Faith. I heard she had gone home to live with her parents. You must be mistaken." Cassandra replied.

"Oh no, it was her all right. You should have seen the look on her face when I walked up to her and said hello. I can't believe she ignored me and walked away without saying a word. She always did think she was somebody special."

Cassandra looked around. Lance had been in the room getting a cup of coffee when Shelley had first started talking, but suddenly disappeared. Hopefully he hadn't heard Shelly's comments.

She whispered," Shelly, you have to keep that information to yourself. Faith is hiding from Lance. She doesn't want anyone to know where she is."

"Oops. Hope I didn't let the cat out of the bag. Do you think he heard me?"

Shelly had a loud shrill voice that carried well. Lance stood outside the door straining to hear more. He heard the words Mi Lei grocery very clearly. Quickly returning to his office, he took the phone book from his desk drawer, but because he wasn't sure of the spelling, it took him quite a long time to find the address of the store.

Each evening, for the next few days he parked on a side street waiting to see her. He must have missed her the first two days, but on the third he saw her walking in the shadows on the opposite side of the street. He followed her in his car for several days noting that she walked the same route every night. Now he knew where she was staying. He should have known that she would be living with Cassandra. When he got the chance he would make Cassandra pay for lying to him when he had asked if she knew where Faith was. Nobody treated him that way and got away with it.

His original plan was to confront Faith then force her into his car, but he had a better idea. One of the streets she crossed was not governed by cross walk lights. He would wait there and, when she began to cross, block her way. She would have to talk to him then.

Cassandra passed along Shelly's comments. Usually Faith was extra cautious walking home, but tonight she was tired. Today was freight day and the girl who usually worked days had called in sick. Faith ended up doing her work as well as her own.

As she stepped off the curb the lights of a car flicked on, blinding her. She heard the sound of a motor being revved up, but by the time she looked to her left, the car was nearly upon her. She tried to run, but stumbled losing her balance. The car swerved and the front fender hit her.

She flew through the air, but just before she hit the pavement she recognized the car as being similar to Lances. The next time she opened her eyes the car was gone and she was surrounded by people.

"Lay still Miss I called an ambulance. It will be here in a few minutes," a voice said. "I saw that car hit you. That driver didn't even try to stop. He has to know he hit something."

Soon a paramedic was leaning over her. She struggled to get to her feet. Two gentle hands restrained her shoulders.

"Don't try and get up. Let us do what we get paid for. Can you tell me your name?" he asked.

"Faith Benson, I am fine, just a bump on the head. I have to get out of here in case he comes back."

"Miss Benson, you have numerous cuts and bruises. We are going to put you in a neck brace and on a back board, then transport you to the hospital. Your arm is broken and you will need stitches to close that cut on your chin. We don't want to take a chance on you having a broken neck so we are going to keep you immobile until we do some x-rays."

Quickly and efficiently she was rolled onto a back board then lifted onto the stretcher.

"Please don't strap down my hands. I can't have them tied down in any way. I get panicky. I promise not to move them" she begged the paramedic as he began tightening the straps around her body.

"OK I'll take your word, but if you become agitated I will have to" he replied. Faith tried to help, but every movement sent a shooting pain up her arm.

Arriving at the emergency department she was amazed at how quickly and efficiently she was looked after. An intern examined her, and then sent her for x-rays of her head, neck, arm and back. He explained that he wouldn't know the extent of the damage done to her until he looked at the films.

After looking at the x-ray films the intern said. "You are a lucky young woman. Your right arm is broken in two places, you need some stitches and you have a concussion. I am going to keep you overnight for observation, but you should be able to go home in the morning if there are no problems. Until then I am going to leave your neck brace on."

He put her arm into a cast and stitched up the cuts on her chin and below her eye. The pain medication made her feel groggy, and she was content to stay where she was.

She noticed a policeman approaching her stretcher. "Can you tell me what happened?" he asked, closing the curtains around the bed for privacy. Taking out his notebook he carefully wrote down everything she said word for word.

"I was walking home from work. I guess the driver didn't notice that I had stepped off the curb."

"Did you see what kind of car it was?"

"No, all I can tell you is that it was white, a sports car I think."

"Can you describe the driver?"

"Everything happened so fast. I don't know."

"Did the driver stop?"

"I don't know. I don't think so. I can't remember."

He took her address and phone number. "We have two eye witnesses to talk with yet tonight. I'll be in back to see you in the morning. Maybe you will be able to remember more once the shock wears off. I understand they are keeping you here tonight for observation. Glad you're OK ma'am."

The Emergency room was very busy. Faith could hear children crying, orders being called out; in all, it sounded like mass confusion. Dozing off in spite of the noise, she became aware of the nurse taking her blood pressure again. She opened her eyes slowly.

"Miss Benson, there is a Mr. Palmer here to see you. I called the emergency contact number you had in your purse."

Faith opened her eyes to see Lance standing beside her bed. At first she thought she was confused "Was Lance driving the car that hit me? I think so but I'm not absolutely sure. Did he try to kill me? "

"Glad to see you're finally awake," he said, bending over and kissing her on the lips. "You gave me quite a scare. I've been standing here for a long time watching you sleep."

"Please, go away. Leave me alone. I don't want you here. I don't want you anywhere near me."

"It's OK Faith; I am going to stay with you until I am sure there are no complications. Then I will take you home so you can rest for a few days," he said taking her hand.

She tried to pull her hand away but he had a firm grip on it. "I'm not going with you"

"I have already arranged with the doctor for you to be released in my care. I am going to look after you," he said, emphasizing the last words.

To an observer these words promised care and support, but to Faith they sounded like a prison sentence. If she went with him, everything she had sacrificed so far would be for nothing. She had already paid dearly to get away from him. She wasn't going with him this time.

She could feel herself drifting in and out of wakefulness. The collar around her neck made it difficult to move. Each time she opened her eyes, Lance was hovering over her. Slowly her mind began to clear. She recalled his words "I will take you home for a few days' rest." Now the burning question in her mind became how was she going to get away from him?

She continued to lay there with her eyes closed, feigning sleep, wishing for an idea or an opportunity that would allow her to escape.

After what seemed like hours later she heard the nurse say, "Mr. Palmer, the Doctor is at the front desk. You said you wanted to talk to him before he discharged Miss Benson. She has had a good night and is stable. He will be releasing her soon."

Lance let go of her hand. She could hear him off in the distance questioning the nurse. "Do you think she remembers much about the accident? Has she said anything to you?"

"No," the nurse replied. "But the police do want to ask a few more questions before she leaves."

Faith panicked. She slid off the stretcher on to her feet and immediately felt so dizzy she could barely stand. "I have to get out of here," she said out loud. "I can't let him take me away from here." She put her hand on the back of the collar tugging at the Velcro straps until they loosened.

With her good hand, she gathered what was left of her clothes and her purse from the chair beside her bed. She felt like she was going to faint. "I can't give in" she told herself. She placed the collar on the stretcher. I'll be fine. The Doctor said my neck wasn't broken that's all that matters."

Peeking out from behind the curtain she saw that the nurses' station was empty. A big commotion was taking place by the doors of the emergency room. She could see Lance standing with his back to her watching what was going on. Getting dressed, especially putting on her jeans, was taking much longer than she expected. She left the hospital gown on, tucking the folds into her waistband. Waves of pain and nausea slowed her down as she tried to button her jacket using only one hand.

While everyone was preoccupied, she slipped through the curtains and began dragging herself down the hallway hanging onto the wall for support. Near the end of the hallway she saw a room marked Maintenance. Pulling open the door she slipped inside.

Through the closed door she could hear loud shouting in the hallway and heard Lance yelling "has anybody seen a young girl with her arm in a cast leave here?"

Then the nurses' voice calmly replied, "I'm sure she hasn't gone too far. She is probably in the washroom. I'll check in there for you."

"You had better find her," Lance continued. "What kind of a hospital do you run here that allows someone in her condition to just get up and walk away?"

"Mr. Palmer, as you can see we are swamped tonight. I checked on her ten minutes ago and she was sleeping. I am sure she hasn't have gone very far."

"I can't let him find me in here "she thought to herself.

Frantically she looked around the Maintenance room for a place to hide. There were metal tiered shelves on two sides of the room, mops and brooms standing in one corner. Then she noticed a narrow space between the end of one shelf and the door. She squeezed into the tiny space, gasping as pain shot through her broken arm. Somehow she managed to tuck that arm behind her so nobody would see the white of the plaster cast if they looked behind the door.

She held her breath when somebody did open the door and looked into the room. Whoever it was didn't see her because the open door concealed her hiding place.

She could hear Lance hollering in the hall way, "You better damn well find her. If you don't, I will sue your asses off."

Faith didn't know how long she hid in her corner. She waited until the hallway was quiet once again. Opening the door, she peeked out and saw the hallway was empty. She slipped out, crept to the end of the corridor then followed a sign that read Front desk. She had no idea where she was. Many times she stopped along the various corridors to lean against the wall and wait for the nausea and dizziness to pass. Eventually she arrived at the front foyer of the hospital. Across from her was a bank of pay phones containing several direct lines to various Taxi firms. There was a gift shop, several offices, a chapel and a sitting area for the patients to wait in. When she was sure there was no one else about, she slipped across the hallway and picked up one of the phones.

"I need a taxi at the main door of Lancaster General."

"About five minutes ma'am."

Staying close to the side wall of the foyer and ducking into the various doorways, she worked her way around to the main entrance. She stood to one side of the open chapel door which gave her a clear view of the drive way but hid her from anyone who walked past. She waited there until her taxi pulled up in front, and then moving as quickly as she could, she went out the front door and slid into the back seat.

 "Please take me to the nearest women's shelter" she asked.

The driver took one look at her battered condition and said "my pleasure ma'am."

Faith leaned her head against the back of the seat with her eyes closed. In what seemed like a short period of time the taxi stopped in front of an ordinary looking house in a quiet subdivision. She rummaged around in her purse looking for enough cash to pay him.

"Don't worry about the money." he said, "the city picks up the tab for these trips." Then he added "I hope they get the guy who did that to you

TWELVE

At first Faith thought the taxi driver was playing a cruel joke on her. He had stopped in front of a two story house which appeared to be the same as all the others on the street, only larger. There were no names or markings to suggest this house was any different than the others.

She looked back at the taxi driver who was standing beside his car watching her. Go ahead he motioned with his hand. Dragging her wounded body up the front steps, she rang the doorbell. The door slowly opened and a woman stepped out.

"Come in dearie," she said waving to the taxi driver. He got back into his taxi and drove away. "You are safe. Nobody will hurt you here."

Putting her arm around Faith's shoulder, she guided her into the house then locked the door and set the alarm behind her. She led her to a small but comfortable office. Pointing to an arm chair she said "you sit here while I go get us something to drink. Would you like tea or coffee?"

"Tea please."

Faith rested her head against the back of the chair and closed her eyes. Tears began flowing down her cheeks; tears of self-loathing, fear, guilt for leaving Josh mixed with self-pity. She heard the lady return to the room and place a warm cup into her hand, then silence. The cleansing tears continued to flow.

Eventually her tears stopped. She opened her eyes and took a sip of her tea. It was cold but she drank it thirstily anyway. The room was a typical office - filing cabinets, a fax machine and a black steel desk over run with paper. On the wall behind the desk was a large golden crucifix. Seeing this, a feeling of peace stole over her. Finally she was safe, but the price had been high and almost cost her life.

"Feeling better now dearie?" the woman asked "My name is Angie Carter and I am the night supervisor."

Faith looked up at her. She saw an older woman, probably early fifties with pure white hair and a little on the plump side. She was dressed in blue jeans and a pink sweat shirt with a teddy bear on the front and she had the kindest gentlest face Faith had ever seen.

"Where am I?" Faith asked.

"Guardian Angels Women's Shelter operated by Catholic Services here in the city."

Handing Faith a clip board she said, "I need you to fill out these forms then I will take you to your room. I have put in a request for the staff nurse to visit you as soon as she arrives in the morning."

Faith was having difficulty filling out the form. She was right handed and it was her right arm that was broken. Mrs. Carter took over for her.

"In your own words can you tell me what happened tonight that brought you here to us?"

"He tried to run me over with his car."

"Who did?'

"My boyfriend, Lance Palmer."

"I hope you reported this to the police."

"Yes, they came to the hospital last night."

"Good, I'll let them know that you are here. They'll probably want to talk to you again in the morning. Is that OK with you?"

"Yes, that will be fine" Faith answered very quietly.

"Come now dearie let's get you to your room. You are obviously hurting and in need of some rest. We can talk some more tomorrow."

The small room was painted a soft pink. Lying on top of the single bed covered with a pink and white quilt was a night gown and house coat. Propped against the head board was a bright pink teddy bear. A table and bed side lamp stood next to the bed and in one corner a reclining arm chair was placed in front of a black metal floor lamp. The wall was adorned with bright pictures of little children playing in the ocean. Off to one side was a bathroom equipped with a shower, toilet and sink. Puffy pink towels hung invitingly on the towel rack. Lined up along the back of the toilet were soap, a tooth brush and all of the personal supplies Faith might need while she was here.

"Do you feel up to having a shower before you go to bed?"

Only then did Faith realize she was filthy. Her jeans and jacket were torn and bloody from landing on the pavement. There was blood in her hair and down the side of her face.

Mrs. Carter helped her undress. She tied a garbage bag around the cast on Faith's arm so that the water couldn't get in, then patiently waited in the bedroom until she was finished.

Faith winced as the warm water touched the open abrasions on her hip and shoulder. Forcing herself to stand there, she let the water cleanse her skin removing the blood and dirt. She was so tired; tired of fighting, tired of running and tired of hurting. She managed to get the night gown on and brush her teeth by herself. Re-entering the bedroom she saw that Mrs. Carter had turned back the covers just like her own mother used to do when she was a little girl. For some reason this kind gesture gave her a feeling of normalcy. She had lived with so much terror the last two years that she had forgotten what was normal and what was not. Gratefully Faith climbed into bed and Mrs. Carter tucked her in leaving the bedside lamp on.

"Oh, by the way Faith, what size are you? I will have to find some different clothes for you to wear. I am going to put these in a plastic bag in case the police need them for evidence." Then she turned off the overhead light and quietly closed the door. Faith fell into a deep dreamless sleep, oblivious that Mrs. Carter checked on her every half hour during the night. To her experienced eye this child had suffered a great trauma before arriving here. She wondered what kind of abuse she had endured..

In the morning Faith felt like she was in a daze. The nurse examined her then called the emergency department and spoke to one of the Doctors. He faxed her records over as well as a prescription for pain medication.

"I think you are doing very well. We have pain medication available, but I don't want you to have any unless the pain in your arm becomes unbearable. Another twenty fours of observation is necessary to be sure there is no bleeding inside your skull." the nurse told her. Then she added "we will take those stitches out in a week. Your other bruises will disappear over time."

Somebody had found her some clothes to wear. She struggled to put on a pair of jeans and a sweat shirt, and then limped down the hallway until she found a lounge. Every bone in her body hurt when she moved. Sitting in an armchair she stared at the world outside through the bars on the window. One of the staff members had brought her a sandwich and a cup of coffee but they remained untouched.

"How did I get myself into this? What do I do now?" she thought, "What was going on in Lance's mind? Did he think I would go back to him willingly?"

Around three that afternoon the police arrived to interview her, again. They were the same two detectives who had questioned her the night Josh was born.

"Can you tell us what happened to bring you here last night?"

With gentle prodding Faith told them the whole sordid story. They sat back and listened, neither one judging her.

"Is this Lance Palmer the same guy who put you into the hospital before?"

"Yes, "Faith admitted. "I was covering up for him. I loved him and his career was just beginning to take off. I didn't want to endanger that."

"Faith" Sandy Rowan said gently "none of this is your fault. He is a predator. He beat you, raped you and tried to run over you. This makes you a victim of abuse. Even if the sex was consensual, and the two of you were living together, that is no excuse for what he has put you through."

"I'm worried about my baby. I haven't seen him for a long time and I am afraid to go near the apartment in case he sees me."

"I'll put in a call to Social Services and have them make a visit to check on him. If he is being well cared for we can't do anything, but if not, the worker will remove him right away.

One more thing, we have recorded our conversation with you. I will get this typed then I want you to read it over very carefully. When you are satisfied, you can sign it. Get one of the ladies who work here to act as a witness. Ordinarily we would have you write everything in your own words, but with your broken arm that isn't possible today. Once your statement is filed, we will arrest Mr. Palmer for attempted murder."

"No" Faith shouted. "I don't want that right now. As long as he has Josh, he can easily follow through with his threat of putting him up for adoption. I can't take a chance on that happening."

After calming her down and assuring her that they would do nothing until she was ready the two left the shelter.

"Don" Sandy Rowan said. "You go back to the precinct office and see if we have anything on this guy. At the same time give this to one of the clerks to transcribe. I'm going to go have a chat with a certain Mr. Lance Palmer."

About an hour later she walked up to the Reception desk of Northrup and Amos and commanded, "I am here to see a Mr. Lance Palmer."

"He is in a meeting right now."

"Get him out," Sandy responded, pulling back her jacket showing Evelyn her police badge. "This is important."

Minutes later a red faced disgruntled Lance Palmer came down the hall. "Detective" he said, "couldn't this have waited. I was in a very important meeting."

"No it could not. Let's go to your office."

Ten minutes later a pale visibly shaken man stood at his office door watching the elevator door close behind Detective Rowan. Nobody knew what had transpired between the two of them.

For the first time in his life, Lance lost his bravado and was afraid. His life and career were beginning to dissolve around him. Faith could ruin him before this was finished.

"That little bitch," he muttered. "I'm going to draw up those adoption papers. She will leave me alone as soon as she realizes I am serious. I am tired of fooling around with her." Then he sauntered back to his meeting acting as if nothing unusual had taken place.

When the meeting was over Lance returned to his office. There was a message waiting for him from Mrs. Murphy, his housekeeper.

"Hi what's up?" he asked. "Is something the matter with Josh?"

"No sir. Social Services came here to check on him. They had a court order so I had to let them in."

"Did they say why?" he asked cautiously.

"No, called it a routine check. Said his mother wanted to make sure he was here and in good condition"

Lance was furious. "I'm going to find her if it's the last thing I do. I'm not going to let her get away with these stupid little games any more. Wait until I get my hands on her, I'll show her once and for all who is the boss." he muttered to himself.

"Mrs. Murphy, I'll be done here in about ten minutes then be on my way home. Why don't you take the evening off? I'll stay with Josh. I have to make some calls that are better made from home."

After Mrs. Murphy left, Lance put Josh to bed and then started phoning. He called every hospital in the city to see if she was there. He badgered Cassandra, but if she knew where Faith was, she wasn't talking. If she was working in a grocery store that meant she was running out of money. He checked her bank account, but nothing had been taken out. Of course there was still the possibility she had opened new accounts, but he didn't think she was smart enough to think of that. He called all five Women's shelters in the city but each told him the same thing, they weren't allowed to give out that information. He called a few of the hotels in the immediate vicinity, but she wasn't registered at any of them.

He paced back and forth. Where was she? He had to find her and soon. If she thought life was bad before, she was going to find out how much worse it could be. That pert little body of hers was going to make him a fortune. As long as he had Josh he could force her into doing anything he wanted. There was no way she was going to take him down, destroy his career and end up with the kid too. He would make her pay.

THIRTEEN

Faith sank into a deep depression completely withdrawing into herself. She followed the rules, kept her room neat and tidy, and met with the various counselors. She performed the duties that were shared among the women at the shelter, but she was oblivious to what was going on around her. Most of the time she stayed in her room, sat in the recliner chair and stared at the wall. The staff was deeply concerned about her, especially Mrs. Carter.

After one of the group counseling sessions she approached Allan Ballard the visiting Psychologist. "Allan I know you are extremely busy, but is there any way you could you fit in a private session with one of our guests, Faith Benson? We aren't getting through to her, she refuses to open up. She is carrying a deep pain within her and frankly I am concerned that she may harm herself."

"I'll try. I do have some free time tomorrow that I can fit her into. Tell me what you know of her story and we'll go from there."

Faith didn't care if she lived or died. Life didn't seem worth living if she had to be alone. The only thought that kept her getting up each morning was that, maybe, somehow she could get Josh back.

Allan Ballard became her life line to sanity. They met twice a week for an hour. After their first session, he diagnosed her with PTSD or Post Traumatic Stress Disorder and began treating her for that condition. She was showing early signs of responding to his treatment.

"I thought that only happened to people who came back from the war." she commented during one of their sessions."

"Not necessarily Faith. This condition can happen to anyone and usually results from having lived through a very traumatic event. Rape victims, like you have a very high incidence of this mental condition. They relive their experience over and over, then begin avoiding going to places that may trigger a memory. Your depression and your history are signs that you are suffering from this. Can you tell me what you are feeling?"

For a long time Faith refused to talk about or deal with her situation during any of their sessions. Sometimes she sat there and said nothing for the full hour. Then slowly, she said one thing and then another. Telling him the details of what Lance had subjected her to was hard on her and often leaving her confused and in a tail spin until the next session, but eventually the whole story came out.

"Faith one way of dealing with this is talking. Another is learning coping skills that will help you work through the fear and anxiety. I'm putting you on some medication that will improve your mood. Once this has started to work I teach you some cognitive behavior exercises and relaxation techniques."

The breakthrough came one day when she said to him "Nobody will ever want me again. I am the most disgusting person on this earth. When I think of some of the things I did for him, and with him I want to run, scream, and hide, but I have no place to go."

"Why are you blaming yourself?"

"I knew better. My excuse was I loved him and I thought he loved me. I wanted to make him happy. I was afraid he would leave me if I didn't do what he wanted. Making sure he was happy became my whole world."

"Faith, this man victimized you. He took advantage of your vulnerability and naivety and I honestly don't think you ever stood a chance. He was a predator who knew exactly what he was doing. You can keep blaming yourself or you can understand that you were not alone. He could have halted these activities at any time. You have been traumatized by the beatings you took. You have been affected not only physically, but mentally and emotionally as well. You need to allow yourself as long as is necessary to heal, and then you will have to learn to forgive yourself."

"I left my son behind. I walked away from him. What kind of a mother does that make me?" she sobbed.

"A smart one! I congratulate you for the courage you showed by doing the right thing at the right time. You had to learn to look after yourself first, before you could be of any value to your son. This act, you think of as being selfish, probably saved your life. When you get stronger, and when the timing is right, nothing will stop you from doing all that you need to do to get your son back. By then, you will be in control of your own feelings and emotions, but until that time comes, you need to be patient with yourself. This will take time. Right now you are having a difficult time coping but I see you getting stronger every time we meet. We still have a lot of work to do, but I promise we will get you to where you feel you can handle your situation."

"Do you really believe that?" she asked.

"Yes I do."

Faith and Cassandra spoke every day. During one their conversations Cassandra mentioned to her that Evelyn had passed along a message for Faith. Her mother had phoned several times wanting to talk to her. Rather than say you no longer worked there Evelyn told her you were in meetings and she would pass along the message, "Honey, you need to call your mother and at least let her know you are alive. She must be worried about you."

Faith knew that she should call her parents and say what? "I turned out to be exactly as dad predicted. " She wasn't quite ready to take that step yet.

Detective Sharp stopped by several times to update her on their investigation. Social Services were making regular visits, and Josh was doing well under Mrs. Murphy's care.

"Faith we have enough information now to charge Lance with attempted murder. A witness came forth who saw what happened that night and got a partial license plate. We have traced that back to Mr. Palmer."

"Not yet please. First I need to find a way to get my son back. I have decided to take him to court for legal custody. After that, you can charge him with anything you want."

Handing her a business card with a phone number hand written on the back he replied. "I want you to call this number. She is a good lawyer, hates men and loves custody cases. I think she can help you."

"Who doesn't hate men?" Faith replied sarcastically.

"Hey, hey, I'm one and I'm on your side." the detective said. For the first time since she had arrived at the shelter Faith giggled.

She couldn't sleep that night. Mrs. Carter was on duty, and after everybody had settled down Faith went to her office. They talked for hours. In spite of everything, and in her own way, she still loved Lance. He was still the father of her child. If she took him to court she may lose, but she would be awarded visiting rights. This was not the best solution, but she knew that once the court had made a decision Lance wouldn't be able to put Josh put up for adoption, he didn't have guts enough to defy the judge's ruling. She also had a choice. She could keep quiet about the money or destroy him.

She paced back and forth in the hallway. By the time the sun rose, she had made up her mind. She was going to do whatever was necessary to get Josh back. If Lance's future was destroyed in the process, so be it. Whether he knew it or not, he was now in the fight of his life. Only one of them would come out a winner.

FOURTEEN

First thing the next morning Faith dialed the number on the card which turned out to be the law office of Martha Simpson.

"Ms. Simpson. My name is Faith Benson. Detective Sharp gave me your card and recommended that I call you."

"Having trouble with a man?"

"Why yes, why do you ask?"

"Only cases I handle. Tell me briefly what I can do for you, and I mean briefly. I have to be in court in thirty minutes"

"I want you to help me get my son back."

"Who has him now?"

"His father"

"We'll talk. Come by my office around three, I should be back by then."

"I can't."

"Look Miss Benson or whatever your name is. I'm too busy for games. Either you will come or you don't want my help. Make up your mind fast."

"I can't come to your office. It is located in the same building as my ex-boyfriends. He is a lawyer who works for Northrup and Amos."

"You afraid you will run into him?"

"Yes."

"Where are you calling from?"

"Guardian Angels Women's Shelter."

"I see, one of those cases. Why didn't you say so at the beginning? Make it known to whoever is on duty that I am coming, and I will try to get there between six and seven. We will talk then" and she abruptly hung up.

Faith was taken back when she saw Martha Simpson. She didn't know what to expect, but certainly not who she saw. She was in her early thirties, a short, slightly dumpy woman dressed in a black suit and black flat lace up shoes. Her hair was severely pulled back into a bun and she wore black horn rimmed glasses.

"Miss Benson I presume" she said extending out her hand to shake Faith's. Then with a twinkle in her eye she said, "This is my no nonsense going to court business costume. I wear this in court to intimidate others but I assure you, I clean up real good."

Faith laughed. She felt very comfortable in the presence of this woman.

"In answer to your questions, I am married and have twin three year old boys plus I am madly in love with my husband."

"Am I that transparent?"

"Yes, actually you are. You couldn't lie if your life depended upon it, your face gives you away. OK let's get started. I hope to get home sometime tonight. You talk, I'll listen and make notes. If I need more information I'll stop you. Start at the beginning."

Martha walked Faith unemotionally through her story, her questions direct and to the point. "First of all I assure you I'm not shocked. I have had to deal with worse than this. Have you told me everything? I get the feeling you are holding out on me, are you?"

"Forgive me Lance" she thought to herself. "You have left me no choice."

"Yes I am. I was hoping not to have to use this information. I promised not to tell, but I have proof hidden away that Lance has stolen tens of thousands of dollars from his clients trust accounts"

"How did you find that out?"

"One of my co-workers came and told me."

"Why?"

"I worked with her in accounting. She came to me because she was worried someone was going to blame her and try to hold her responsible for the missing money."

"Why would she think that?"

"She has access to and signing authority on every account. Someone had to be able to get her password in order to get into the accounts."

"Do you think she is guilty?"

"No. I'm sure she isn't."

"How can you be so sure?"

"After she told me she thought Lance was taking the money from the accounts I decided to look into matters myself. For the better part of two weeks I stayed after everyone left and checked the files. She was right. The only accounts missing money were Lances. I photocopied the files I thought were relevant then entered them into a computer program I have on my lap top. When I was finished I could see that tens of thousands of dollars were missing. I copied all of that information onto a flash drive then hid everything."

"Where are those files now?"

"In my office."

"Out of everything you have told me this evening that is the only time you have used that pretty little head of yours."

Faith was instantly angry. "You don't have any right to make those kinds of comments about me. I don't appreciate them."

"Well get used to them. If we take on this case it's going to get a lot worse than that. As your lawyer I want facts and truth. When you had this information why didn't you report him to the head of your firm? That makes you look as guilty as he may be."

"I know. I wanted to tell Lance first that I knew what was going on and give him an opportunity to make things right and put the money back. The evening I confronted him was the same evening he put me in the hospital; the night Josh and I both nearly died."

"Yet you went back to him. That wasn't smart on your part."

"I know, but I loved him. I had no place to go. I thought because we had a baby together things would change, that we would get married someday. What a fool I was."

"Leave this with me for a few days and I'll get back to you sometime next week. I think you and I are going to make that sucker sorry he ever set eyes on you. You know Faith, I really don't hate men, I just hate the way they think that they can push us around because we are women."

A full week passed before Martha contacted Faith again. "I need those files. Can you get them for me?"

Faith hesitated. In her heart she knew that giving Martha the files would be the end of her relationship with Lance.

"What's the matter? Can you get them or not?"

"Martha this is so hard. I still love him. He will always be Josh's father. Maybe if he got help he could change, maybe one day we could still be happy together."

"Girl, the time has come for you to take a reality check. I understand that you still have deep feelings for him. They may never go away, but Faith, the reality is he beat you up and nearly killed you and your baby. For heaven's sake, you are living in a Women's shelter, afraid to go out, living in constant fear that he will find you. The truth Faith is that he used you for his own gratification. When he was tired of you he would have tossed you aside like a piece of garbage and gone on to the next young girl stupid enough to fall for his line. You never stood a chance against him. Stop living in your little dream world, and wake up and smell the coffee. He doesn't love you and probably never did. It's as plain and simple as that."

"He will never change will he?"

"No, that's the way he is. You have to make a choice now, him or a life with your son. Either way there is no going back. If you decide you want to be with Lance, you might as well move out of the shelter today and crawl back to him. If you give me the files we will use those against him. If we can prove what you say, then he will be disbarred and possibly go to jail for fifteen years. What's it going to be?"

"I guess I'll get you the files. Lance is going to hate me for doing this to him."

"I can't argue with that. Is there somebody in your office that you trust enough to get those files and not tell Lance?"

"Yes. I'll have her bring them to you."

"Good girl, you are finally starting to grow up and make some adult decisions. Faith I know this isn't easy, but keep telling yourself that you are doing this because it is necessary to get your son back."

Faith waited until lunch hour was over and she knew Carole would be back in her office.

"Hi Carole Faith Benson here. I need your help. You have to trust me and do exactly as I say. Please don't ask any questions or tell anyone that I called and asked you to do this for me."

"Sound kind of mysterious to me." replied Carole.

"Will you do this for me even if you don't know what is going on?"

"Sure."

"In the back of your filing cabinet behind the Z's is a file folder with my name on the front. Take that and put it into a brown envelope. Don't look at what's inside. That way, if you are ever asked, you can truthfully say that you didn't know. Then, go into my office and taped to the top shelf of the closet is a flash drive. Put that into the same envelope, then deliver the whole package to Martha Simpson's office on the twenty-second floor."

"No problem. How are you doing Faith?"

"Hanging in, but after I know that Martha has that file I am going to be doing a whole lot better Oh and Carole, thank you. This means a lot to me."

Within days Faith moved out of the shelter into a secure apartment complex located on the same lot. Her apartment was fully furnished with comfortable used furniture. The purpose of the move was to begin integrating her back into everyday life. She could stay until she had a job or another place to go. For Faith, this meant that she was finally able to start over. Still she was very cautious. According to Cassandra Lance was still trying to find her.

She was getting impatient too. Once again she was waiting to hear from Martha. She had left several messages, but her calls hadn't been returned. She was also painfully aware that patience wasn't one of her strongest virtues.

Faith jumped when her phone rang. Martha and Cassandra were the only people who had her phone number, but there had been a couple of crank calls several days ago. She was worried that somehow Lance had found her phone number and was making sure she was home.

"Hello," she said cautiously.

"Got to talk fast, I'm on my way back to my office from the court house. Anyway, after looking at those files you gave me, I realized there is more to this than meets the eye. This man isn't about to let you to have you son back without a fight. He doesn't want him, but as long as Josh is in his care or under his control, he will use him to keep you quiet. We already know how far he will go if he feels threatened.

I took it upon myself to set up a meeting with Northrup and Amos. I wanted them to have this information before we go to court. Naturally they were very upset. They didn't want the information about the missing money to get out, especially when they weren't sure where the money disappeared to or who was responsible. Their first concern is protecting their own reputations and that of the firm. I can understand that. They have spent a lifetime building a reputation, and they don't want someone to tear it out from underneath them.

Mr. Amos questioned me intensely as to why you hadn't brought this information to their attention when you first found out. They were quite shocked when I told them how you were abused by this man, and that he was continuing to harass you. You know you should have gone to them first."

"I know, but at the time I wanted to give Lance a chance to put the money back or admit his guilt. I wanted to convince him to stop before he got caught."

"Mr. Amos felt especially bad. He was the one who convinced his partners to hire Lance. He was doing it as a favor to Lance's father. They had gone to college together. Apparently Lance had a few problems in University with drugs. His dad wanted him to work in a place that would provide him with a good foundation and work ethic. He thought that, if they kept him busy enough, he wouldn't have time to continue that foolishness.

He turned out to be a brilliant lawyer. He works hard when he is working, and is successful. He was their golden boy, their chief money maker. They had big plans for him.

Mr. Northrup was so angry he wanted to call Lance into the office immediately and fire him. I convinced them that they would be better leaving him where he is so they can keep an eye on him. I wanted them to understand that, by firing Lance, they would be putting both you and Josh in danger. I had to do some fast talking, but finally they agreed.

I also talked them into hiring Big Ed Finley, a Private Investigator I work with, Big Ed Finley is his name. I told them he would find out as much as he could about their Mr. Palmer. I got Big Ed started yesterday."

"Martha, stop. I can't afford any of this. I have some money but not enough to cover all these expenses."

"I talked to them about that too. If, in your custody hearing there is some way that Lance confesses to taking the money, they will cover all of my costs including Big Ed and pay for your custody battle. I convinced them that, without your help and your evidence, they would have never found out who was guilty. They have insurance to cover the theft but they will not get paid until someone has been arrested and convicted."

Faith didn't know how to respond. This all seemed too good to be true.

"One more thing Faith, part way through our discussion they asked a lady by the name of Elizabeth Heatley to join us. Do you trust her? Does she know your story?"

"Yes on both counts. In fact, she was the one who suggested that I may have to leave Josh in Lance's care. She made me realize I needed to look after myself first before I would be in any position to look after Josh."

"Good. I was hoping you trusted her. She is going to be our eyes and ears at the office. One more thing Faith, I know how conflicted you are. I am aware that you think you are still in love with Lance, that you feel you owe him something, but he can't find out about this. If he does, I fear for you and Josh. If he is really determined to find you he could within a short period of time. Who else knows where you are?"

"Cassandra, and my parents."

"Tell them not to say anything to anybody or answer any questions about you. If somebody gets overly nosey, they should refer them to me. We need you in court."

After she hung up the phone Faith thought, "finally things are beginning to move forward but I didn't plan on destroying Lance in the process."

Faith had also taken the bold step of phoning Mrs. Murphy, Josh's babysitter. After her initial reticence they got along well.

"Why don't you come and see him one day here at the apartment. It will be good for the two of you to get re-acquainted once again. That little boy needs his mother." urged Mrs. Murphy.

After several such requests Faith told her "I can't. I can only guess what you have been told about me, but I am hiding from Lance. I can't take a chance on him finding out I was there."

Mrs. Murphy seemed to ignore Faith's comment. "Josh likes to go to Simmons Park. I take him there once or twice a week. In fact, I am planning on going tomorrow morning. He likes playing on the swing and the slide. We usually get there around ten and stay for about an hour."

Faith understood her message. The next morning she dressed in a pair of old jeans and a sloppy white sweat shirt. She pinned her auburn hair to the top of her head, then added a white baseball cap. To complete her disguise she put on a pair of dark sunglasses.

Six months had passed since she had last seen Josh. Her heart ached to hold him in her arms once again. She couldn't begin to imagine how much he had changed. Would he still remember her?

The closer she got to Simmons Park, the more anxious she became. "What if this is a trap? What if Lance is waiting for me? I wouldn't put it past him to try something like this." she thought.

She arrived early and waited on a park bench on the far side of the playground. "This way, if something doesn't feel right, I can still leave without being seen. If Lance is anywhere nearby I'll see him before he sees me."

At exactly ten o'clock an older woman came to the playground pushing a stroller. She picked up the little boy and took him over to the swings. After a while the woman and little boy began walking on the grass, moving closer to where Faith sat.

Her heart ached to see him playing there. How he had grown. She wanted to run to him, scoop him up into her arms, and cover his little face with kisses.

The woman sat down beside her on the bench, then lifted Josh up onto her knee. She said nothing, neither did Faith. She sat staring at her son. It had been such a long time. She held his little hand and they played a game of peek- a- boo. A casual observer might have thought they were a mother and grandmother spending time in the outdoors.

At eleven o'clock exactly, the woman picked up the little boy and began walking back across the grass to the stroller. Faith whispered to her "thank you." The woman didn't reply.

Faith watched them until they left the playground. She felt as if her heart was breaking in two. Just before they disappeared from view the woman turned and waved

Looking at the empty pathway, she whispered "I am coming for you little one. Soon I hope."

The two women formed a bond of conspiracy. Every Tuesday morning Faith met Mrs. Murphy and Josh at the park. She played with Josh, pushing him on the swings, helping him up the slide, and then catching him at the bottom. Together they built roads in the sand box and she wiped his tears when he fell.

When they were together Mrs. Murphy was a woman of few words. She watched Josh like a hawk making sure Faith did nothing that would hurt him. In public they were wary of each other, but had long conversations on the phone several times a week.

As the court date approached Faith suggested to Mrs. Murphy "perhaps it would be better if I stop coming. I don't want Lance to find out and for your job to be in jeopardy. If he wins custody, I know that as long as Josh is with you he is in good hands."

Mrs. Murphy thought for a minute then replied "perhaps you are right. Good luck Faith. This little boy loves you. He really should be with his mother."

"This mother needs to be with her son too" she replied, her eyes filling with tears.

Martha returned her call a few days later. "We have a family court date six weeks from now with Judge Harrison. But there is one thing we need to ask you to do."

"What's that?"

"We want you to go to Lance's office and inform him that you intend to get your baby back. The court needs evidence that you have tried."

"I can't."

"At the same time, we want you to get him to admit what he knows about the missing money. This will back up your story about why he put you in the hospital the night Josh was born.

"Martha I can't go to his office. Please don't ask me to."

"Look, if you want to get your son back, you have to get your hands dirty. The time for playing nice is over. My office, Thursday morning. Faith, we will watch out for you. I promise we will keep you safe. You have to trust that we know what we are doing."

Thursday morning, a frightened anxious Faith Benson once again walked through the office tower doors.

"Good morning Andrew," she said "I'm on my way to Martha Simpson's office."

"Why Faith Benson, how are you. Good to see you again." he said, smiling broadly at her. "I miss seeing you around here."

"I miss coming to work every day too," Faith replied.

By the time she reached the twenty second floor she was shaking like a leaf. When the elevator door opened Martha was waiting for her.

'Faith," she said. "Be strong. Work with us on this. We know you are scared, but we need this. In order to prove our case we need to show you tried to get your son back, that you didn't merely abandon him. We have to show the court that you had a good reason for leaving as you did. We want to be able to prove that you had to choose between being with your son in an obsessive controlling relationship or building a better life for the two of you. Focus on the fact that what you do today will go a long way in getting your son back.

I have witnesses lined up to support the distress you were in, but we need to hear him actually threaten you. That scum bag doesn't deserve to walk on this earth."

Faith laughed. "I couldn't have said it better myself." The tension in the room was broken.

"I want you to meet "Big Ed" my husband. This was his idea. He is a licensed private detective and used to doing Underhanded things like this." Big Ed smiled back affectionately at his wife.

Big Ed was not as big as his name suggested. He was a little over six feet tall and muscular. It was evident he spent part of his time lifting weights. The muscles of his thick arms and chest filled out the black tee shirt he was wearing. He had rugged good looks but his nose was slightly crooked. Faith wondered how many times it had been broken, once for sure.

He helped Faith fit a voice activated recorder to the waistband of her slacks and then threaded the wire across her back and over her shoulder. This was then attached to a Rose pin on the lapel of her jacket. The rose was actually a tiny microphone. When he was satisfied he accompanied her to the sixteenth floor.

"Good morning Evelyn. Is Lance in his office?" she asked.

"Faith Benson, how are you? Should I tell him you are here?"

"No, thank you, I want to surprise him."

She was so intent on her purpose that she didn't see Elizabeth Heatley standing in the doorway of her office. She walked down the hall, then without knocking, walked into his office.

"I told you not to bother me. Can't you see I am busy," he snarled, not looking up from the stack of papers on his desk.

"Hi Lance ,are you too busy to see me?" Faith said sweetly. "It's been a long time."

He looked up, his face revealing the shock he felt. In two steps he was at her side, his arms reaching for her.

"Where have you been? I have been looking all over for you" ' he said huskily, trying to pull her into his embrace.

She backed away from him. If he kissed her, she would lose her resolve. Just the sound of his voice made her feel weak in the knees. All she wanted to sink into his arms, but if she allowed herself one second of weakness, she would lose all she was fighting for. In spite of everything that had transpired between them, she could go back to him with open arms.

"I have come to take Josh back."

He looked at her with disdain. "So that's why you suddenly decided to show up. Do you really think that you can waltz in here, demand our son, and believe I will hand him over just like that? Guess again, because there is no way in hell that is going to happen."

"I am his mother and I have every right to see and be with him. Besides I have come to offer you a deal."

"You gave up your rights when you left us on the ferry. What kind of deal? What are you going to offer me, use of your hot little body? Girls like you are a dime a dozen. I can get any one of them I want, any time I want, with no strings attached, so I hope you have something better than that."

"I am here to offer you my silence about the money you have been stealing from your client's accounts. In this envelope are the files I copied on to a flash drive and the photocopies I made. I will sign a non-disclosure agreement and go work at another firm. All I ask is that you let me have Josh in exchange."

Lance stared to laugh." Did you really think I would fall for that? Your fancy files and flash drive won't do you any good. I have the password and moved the enough money around so there is no evidence that any was missing from my accounts in the first place. I do believe that two other guys will have a lot of explaining to do. Their accounts are short," he sneered.

"Know what? I think I will pick up this phone, call the police and charge you with extortion. How does that sound? Maybe, while we are waiting for them to come, we can lock the door and make up for lost time. You know, once more for old times' sake. Why we could even watch a video if you prefer. Do you remember the night we made those? No, of course not, I made sure of that. You are very photogenic when you are naked. Maybe we could make some more. I might make some sort of a deal if you wanted to go for that. Better still, you come back to me, do what I want and you will have your precious son back."

"Do you mean move back in with you? Lance I can't do that."

"Then no deal."

"Lance please," Faith begged "I have to be able to see him, to be with him. I want to watch him grow up. I am still his mother."

"Not in this life time baby, my way or the highway. I should have finished the job when I hit you with my car, would have saved us both a lot of grief."

Then, reaching into his desk drawer, he pulled of a sheaf of papers and threw them at her. "Take a good look. These are signed adoption papers. All I have to do is walk through the court house door and you will never see him again. Now give me that flash drive and get out of here."

"Lance please" she begged, and then realized her words were of no use. Something inside her turned as cold as ice. "You don't leave me any other choice. I will fight you with everything I have. See you in court."

"Hope you have more than this. This proves nothing." he retorted.

Faith opened the door, stared at him for a long second and walked out. As soon as the door closed she slumped against the wall, sliding down to the floor. She could hear the sound of his laughter through the door. She was trembling violently. Silently she prayed that this had worked, that there was enough evidence on the tape to convince a judge her son wasn't safe with that man.

A gentle hand touched her on the shoulder and helped her to her feet. It was Mrs. Heatley.

"Come Faith, you need to leave here as quickly as you can."

Faith looked at her through tear filled eyes and said "I did it"

Mrs. Heatley replied. "You sure did. I'm proud of you Faith, this couldn't have been easy. I knew you had hidden strength all along, that's why I put you on probation."

She took Faith by the arm, led her to the elevator and stayed with her until the door closed.

Faith pushed the up button and got off at the twenty second floor. Martha and Big Ed were waiting for her. Without a word she removed the microphone and tape recorder, the distress of what had taken place written all over her face.

Instinctively she knew Mrs. Heatley was right, she had to get out of here before Lance came looking for her. He could already be downstairs, waiting for her to come out of an elevator.

Getting off the elevator on the second floor she walked down the stairs to the lobby. Once on the main floor she rushed over to Andrew and said "Please call me a taxi and tell them to hurry. This is an emergency."

Andrew did as he was asked. He liked Faith, and found it hard to believe the rumors and innuendo that were circulating about her. Seeing the terrified look on her face made him feel that he needed to protect her.

"Come, stand back here with me until your taxi gets here. At this time of day it shouldn't take very long."

When the taxi pulled up in front Andrew took her arm and escorted her safely to the car. As the taxi was pulling away from the curb, Lance came running out the double doors onto the sidewalk. Faith didn't see him.

"Where to ma'am?" The driver asked.

"Guardian Angels Women's shelter please."

FIFTEEN

Safely back in her apartment Faith locked her door and closed all of the curtains leaving a space big enough to allow her to see the street below. She sat there watching the traffic go by, terrified that somehow Lance had followed her.

She huddled in one corner of the sofa, her nerves as tight as a steel drum, jumping at every sound she heard, her mind racing with terrible thoughts of what he would do if he found her. Several hours later she realized he wasn't coming. She closed the curtains all the way then picked up the phone and dialed her mother's number.

"Mom, I want to let you know what I am doing. I have hired a lawyer and I am taking Lance to court for custody of Josh. You may hear or read many things about me if the newspapers get hold of the story. I want you and dad to be prepared because this could get very nasty."

"Do you want me to come and be with you?"

"No, I can handle this on my own. Please try and understand that. I don't want either you or dad mixed up in this. This is my fight."

"You know that I don't agree with you. I can't for the life of me understand why you think that you have to do this alone? You do whatever you think is necessary so we get that little boy back."

"Mom, how is dad handling all of this? Is he there? Do you think he will talk to me?"

"He isn't here Faith. He's gone to a meeting, but I will tell him you called."

"Is he still mad at me?"

"He'll get over it. You get that little boy back do you hear. Love you."

"Love you too mom" Faith replied, and then hung up the phone.

Glancing at the call display she saw that Martha had called twice but decided not to call her back. She needed some time to think. Sitting on the sofa, looking out through the now open curtains she watched the day fade into evening. There were no answers to her questions. How had her life ended up this way? What was she going to do if she lost Josh forever?

After weeks of anxiety and preparation, the day had finally come. She was going to court to fight for her son. Her mood matched the weather outside, gloomy and dull. After today her life would begin anew, either with her son or he would be lost to her forever. She had no doubt that if Lance received custody of Josh he would do everything possible to keep her away. Depending upon the court's decision, there was a distinct possibility she might not see him again.

She dressed carefully remembering Mrs. Heatley's advice about looking professional. The day before, she had gone to a second hand store that sold used business clothing for women, and purchased a new ivory colored suit. Her only accessory was a string of pearls.

The plan was to meet Martha in a small conference room at the court house two hours before their scheduled time to go over some of the minor details of her case. The taxi Martha had ordered seemed to take forever and she wished the day was over.

Martha had repeatedly told her to be prepared for the custody hearing to get ugly but she hoped it wouldn't. She was afraid of what may be dragged into the public spotlight. Deep in her heart Faith was convinced that Lance truly did love her, and In the end, he would realize what he stood to lose and back down.

With a heavy heart she walked slowly up the stairs to the second floor of the court house, counting each step like she used to do when she was a child. There were forty two. She didn't want to be here. At the top she faltered, immediately recognizing the man getting up off a bench by the court room door. It was her father.

"Oh no," she moaned. "I don't need him here today. I won't be able to stand him preaching at me with his arrogant I told you so attitude."

Clive Benson watched his daughter come up the stairs and saw her hesitate when she saw him. He rose from the bench and slowly began walking toward her. Instinctively she ran toward him. He opened his arms and she ran into them.

"Oh daddy, I am so sorry you have to be here." she sobbed," but I am glad you came. I have missed you so much."

Clive cried as he held his daughter in his arms. He led her over to a bench where they sat down side by side. He put his arm around her shoulders and held her tightly.

"Why did you come? How did you find out? Is mom with you?"

"Slow down Faith, one question at a time. No, your mom isn't here. In fact she doesn't even know I'm here. I took the day off work and drove in early this morning. I couldn't let my baby girl go through an ordeal such as this alone."

Looking straight into her eyes he said "Faith, I haven't had a drink in over six months, ever since the night you called me a foul mouth self-serving drunk. I have been going to AA meetings three times a week to stay sober."

"Dad, I didn't call you that."

"I know, not in those exact words, but you were right. You made me realize what I had become. When I looked in the mirror I didn't like what I saw."

"Dad, there's my Lawyer Martha Simpson. I have to meet with her before court starts. Come and meet her. She is an amazing woman."

Taking her dad by the hand they went to greet her. Faith made the introductions, then Martha said. "Thank you for taking my advice and coming Mr. Benson. Faith needs someone who loves her here today."

"Did you ask him to come?" Faith asked.

"Yes. Whether you agree or not is not my problem. I decided that you needed your parents during an ordeal like this. They need to be able to support their only daughter when she is in trouble. I put myself in their position, and decided that if you were my daughter I wouldn't let you go through this alone."

Faith came face to face with Lance at the door of the court room. He barely glanced at her. He sat down at a table on the right side of the court room to confer with his lawyer; she went to the table on the opposite side. She didn't recognize his lawyer. He was someone from outside the firm, probably and another one of Lance's sleazy friends. Her dad sat down on the bench immediately behind her. At the back of the court room sitting on one side were Mr. Amos, Cassandra and Mrs. Heatley. Detective Don Sharp sat alone on the other. Knowing that they were sitting there, supporting her, made her feel stronger.

Judge Harrison, an imposing figure in his black robe and white hair, entered the court room and took his place. Faith took a deep breath. Whatever happened here would determine the rest of her life.

"This is my family court. I am Judge Ronald Harrison. I like to keep the proceedings rather informal but don't forget this is a court of law. My decision will concern only what I think is best for the child Josh Benson. Shall we begin? You first Mr. Palmer, tell this court why you think you are the person best suited to care for the child."

Lance and his lawyer moved to a chair located at the front of the courtroom right next to the judge's stand. Lance was sworn in by the clerk. Even in her worst moments Faith had not anticipated the type of questions asked by his lawyer, nor Lance's answers.

"Mr. Palmer. You're currently caring for the infant Josh Benson. Is that correct?"

"Yes."

"Tell this court how that came to be."

"Faith and I were on the ferry returning from a Corporate weekend on Devil's Island. The company always gives us a holiday with our family for a few days each year as a way of saying thank you. The ferry was getting ready to dock and she disappeared. She simply walked away, leaving Josh with me and didn't look back. I have absolutely no idea why she did this or what was going on in her head at the time. Later, when she was hit by a car I went to pick her up at the hospital, but she ran away from there also. I didn't see or hear from her again until two months ago when she walked into my office, making a scene and demanding full custody."

"How did you first meet Miss Benson?"

"At a bar, then a short time later she was assigned to work with me preparing for a civil lawsuit."

"Tell us about Miss Benson. How did she present herself to you?"

"At first she put on the innocent little school girl act, but she turned out to be anything but. Later I found out she was a drunk and heavily involved with drugs."

"What else can you tell us?"

"I hate to say this but she was a pretty free and easy with her body. I couldn't resist the sex she offered me. Why pay, when what you want is offered free on a silver platter," he smugly replied.

Someone in the court room giggled. Judge Harrison frowned.

"Tell us about the night your son Josh was born."

"When I arrived home from work the paramedics were working on getting her stabilized. She had been badly beaten, was unconscious and was bleeding from down below. At first I wasn't sure if she was going to survive."

"Do you have any idea who would have done this to her?"

"Not really. I thought it might be one of the drug dealers she owed money to."

Faith jumped to her feet. "He is lying. None of this is true."

Martha grabbed her arm and pulled her back onto her chair.

Judge Harrison reprimanded her. "Miss Benson, you will have an opportunity to refute what he says later. Try to remain calm and let him explain his side of the story."

Lances' lawyer continued. "Were you concerned for her after the baby was born?"

"Yes. The baby was born by caesarean section a month early. I took her back into my home because I felt sorry for her. I was worried about the baby's welfare."

"As a result of her leaving you with the child, what arrangements have you had to make?"

"I had to hire a full time live in house keeper to look after Josh. I also pay premium rates to put him in the office day care when she has a day off. I have already made arrangements for him to go into a private pre-school program when he is three."

"Can you afford these additional expenses?"

"Not really, but I find a way. It is important that Josh have a stable home environment to grow up in. At least I can feed and clothe him. I can't do anything about how his mother treats him, but at least I know I will be here to support him."

"One last question Mr. Palmer, Is Josh your son?"

"I don't know for sure. Faith says he is. When she was high and drunk she would have sex with anyone who came along. She wasn't fussy. I hope he is mine, and I'm going to try and do the best I can for him."

"Mr. Palmer. I know this is difficult, but did you witness Faith Benson acting in the manner you just described?"

"Yes, we were at a get together one night with a couple guys from the office. She was both, high and drunk, right out of control. The next thing I knew she was doing a strip tease on the table. I left to use the men's room, and when I came back she was naked and screwing some guy on the sofa in front of everybody. She was so out of it that night, that if I hadn't stepped in, she would have willingly taken on every guy in the room. "

"How many others were there?"

"Four, besides me."

"How did you feel about this?

"I was disgusted. Shortly after that I asked her to move out. She refused, begged me to stay and I let her. Two months later she informed me she was pregnant. I don't know if Josh is my kid, but I love him as if he were."

"One more thing did you and Miss Benson have sexual relations that same night or any time after that?"

"Yes."

"So it is possible Josh is your son?"

"Yes."

"That is all Mr. Palmer. Thank you for your direct and sincere testimony. I know how hard it must be for you to stand up here and reveal the true character of the woman who is the mother of your child. I am sure it is quite evident to this court that she often acts in an irresponsible manner. "

"I think that if she had to choose between drugs and the baby, the drugs would win," Lance added.

"Miss Simpson. You have something you wish to say?" asked Judge Harrison.

"Yes sir. May we have a ten minute recess while I confer with my client?"

"Court will reconvene in ten minutes."

Faith was sobbing and ashamed. Lance had made her sound like the filthiest, most depraved woman on this earth. She couldn't turn around and look at her father's face after him hearing that. Everything Lance had said, in his convoluted way, was based upon an element of truth. She felt like a whore.

"One thing for sure," she thought "he enjoyed himself each time I offered myself to him."

In the small conference room Martha encouraged her. "Now it's your turn to tell what really happened. Tell the truth, only answer my questions, and don't add anything else. Oh, and turn off those damn tears, they make you look as guilty as hell. You are in a fight for your reputation, and this is the only opportunity you are going to have to get that and your son back. Make the most of it."

Exactly ten minutes later Judge Harrison came back into the court room. "Your turn Miss Benson, tell me why you should have custody of your son."

Faith got up from behind the table and walked to the chair at the front of the court room. She sat staring at the floor too embarrassed to look up as the clerk swore her in.

"Miss Benson, tell the court where you met Mr. Palmer," Martha began.

"The first time was at the Crown and Anchor Pub. My roommate and I had gone there to hear the live band performing that night."

"Were you drunk?"

"No, but I had consumed several drinks."

"Did you and Mr. Palmer work intimately together on a law suit for a long period of time?"

"Yes."

"Did you sleep with him during this time?"

"Yes. I didn't mean to, but I fell in love with him. Things just happened."

"Were you a virgin up until that night?"

"Yes, he seduced me."

"Is it true, that the two of you did a great deal of partying and drugs?"

"Yes"

"Did you have sex with another in Mr. Palmer's presence?"

"Yes. Lance was watching the whole time. He didn't leave the room like he said."

"Were you fully aware of your actions that night?"

"No."

"Did Mr. Palmer attempt to discourage or protect you?"

"No,"

"What was his reaction to all of this?"

"He said he enjoyed my performance, and that next time he would join in."

"Was there a next time?"

"No."

"What was the end result of that discussion?"

"I haven't had a drink or done any drugs since then. When I sobered up, I was humiliated and ashamed. I realized I had sunk so low there was no place left to go."

"What was the reason for your behavior that evening?"

"I was angry. Mrs. Heatley, our office manager, had called me into her office and said she was going to have to let me go. I begged her not to and was put on probation for three months. I didn't want to lose my job."

"Miss Benson, in your best recollection, how many men have you had sex with?"

"Two. Lance and the man that night. I was a virgin the first time Lance and I made love."

"Miss Benson, take us back to the first time Mr. Palmer beat you up.

"I can't Martha. Please don't ask me to. "

"You must. Tell us in your own words what happened."

"I found a note from another woman in his shirt pocket as well as lipstick on his collar. We were living together at the time, but not getting along very well."

"How did this make you feel?"

"Angry and betrayed. I waited up for him to come home then confronted him with the evidence. I wanted to find out who she was."

"What happened then?"

"He had been drinking, and I think he was also high. We argued. He grabbed me by my hair and dragged me around the apartment, banging my head against the floor and the wall. He kicked me in the stomach and punched me in the face. I tried to hide in the bathroom, but he forced his way in, whipped me with his belt, raped me, and as he was leaving spit on me."

She looked up at her dad. He was pale, his face a mask of shock and despair. He could not meet her eyes.

"Yet you went back to him?"

"Yes. I loved him. He told me he had blacked out and didn't remember anything. He promised to never hit me again. He brought me dozens of red roses to say he was sorry. I believed him."

"Is that about the time you got pregnant?

"Yes."

"How long was this after you had been involved with the other man?"

"Two months. I wasn't pregnant because of him." She looked at Lance and said "you knew that. We were both relieved to find out nothing had happened that night."

"Miss Benson, were you using any form of contraception?"

"Yes, I was on the pill, but kept forgetting to take them on a regular basis."

"Why did he beat you that particular night?"

"He came home and informed me he had invited his friends over on Friday evening and I was their entertainment. They were each paying him two hundred dollars for the booze, drugs and me. I told him that I wasn't going to prostitute myself for him or anybody else, and that he had better forget that idea."

"You asked Mr. Palmer to marry you did you not?"

"Yes."

"What was the result of that discussion?"

"He refused. He called me names, said I was the last person he would want."

"Yet all of this time he was encouraging you to entertain his friends?"

"Yes."

"When you told Mr. Palmer you were pregnant how did he react?"

"He told me to get rid of the baby. He wanted me to have an abortion but I refused."

"Now let's move forward. Did Mr. Palmer ever beat you again?"

"Yes."

"When?"

"The night Josh was born. He had been drinking, we argued. Then he knocked me down and kicked me repeatedly in the stomach."

"Why?"

"Martha please, I promised Lance........."

"Faith, you are under oath. You have no choice."

"A co-worker, Carole Adams, had confided in me that thousands of dollars were missing from his clients' accounts. I wanted to warn him, as well as find out if what she said was true. I wanted him to put the money back and stop before he got caught and ended up going to jail."

"You investigated these allegations on your own time. What did you find?"

"Carole was telling the truth."

"Now we are going to talk about when you deserted your son on the ferry. What prompted this decision?"

"I was afraid. We had been to Devil's Island for the annual Corporate Retreat. Lance was expecting to receive an offer for a full partnership with the firm. When he didn't get it he was very angry. He blamed me, said it was my fault because I deliberately got pregnant to make him look bad. I couldn't stand to take another beating like the previous two. I was afraid that one of these times he wouldn't stop until I was dead."

"What happened the next time you saw him?"

"I am sure he was driving the car that hit me. I broke my arm and had a concussion."

"Then what happened"

"The hospital called him to come and take me home because I had him listed as my emergency contact number. I didn't want to go with him, so I hid in the Maintenance room. He created a big scene. When the nurse escorted him out, I ran around to the front door, phoned for a taxi and went to a women's shelter.

"You saw him recently did you not?"

"Yes. I went to his office."

"Tell us about that."

"I went to bargain with him. I wanted my son back. I had a copy of the original flash drive with me which contained the records of all the money missing from his clients' accounts. I was willing to trade that and sign a non-disclosure agreement if he would give me Josh."

"What else happened?"

"He had adoption papers filled out in his desk drawer. He said all he had to do was file them with the court, and I would never see my son again. I gave him the flash drive anyway. He also told me that if I came back to him, I would have full access to Josh. He threatened me with a video he made and which I knew nothing about. One weekend he drugged me and I still can't remember anything that took place I never once thought that he was capable of doing something like that to me.

134

"Miss Benson, is it true that you were wearing a tape recorder and taped your conversation the day you went to Mr. Palmer's office?"

"Yes."

Lance jumped to his feet in protest. His lawyer made him sit down.

Martha handed a tape to Judge Harrison and one to Lance's lawyer. "This is a copy of that recorded conversation."

"Thank you Miss Benson, you may go back to your chair now."

Lance's lawyer stood up. "I would like to ask Miss Benson a couple of questions Your Honor."

"Go ahead," replied Judge Harrison.

"How many men did you have sex with before Mr. Palmer?"

"I already answered that. None, he was the first."

"Did you perform a sexual act with another man at a party while Mr. Palmer looked on?"

"Yes."

"How many more times did this occur? Were you high on drugs at the time?"

"That was the only time. Yes, I had been snorting lines of cocaine all evening.

"Did you refuse Mr. Palmer's offer to help you get an abortion? Did you threaten him that you were going to make him pay for the rest of his life?"

"Yes I said that."

"One more question. If you think my client tried to run over you, why didn't you press charges when the police wanted you to?"

"I wanted my son back. I was afraid Lance would carry through on his threat to put him up for adoption."

"Are you sure it was Mr. Palmer driving the car that hit you?"

"Yes."

"One final question, how will you support your son if you get custody?"

"I am a Legal Assistant. I make good money when I am working. I will be able to afford having him with me."

"Are you expecting Mr. Palmer to pay you a monthly sum of money for child support?"

"Yes." Faith had been pushed too far. "I didn't get pregnant by myself. Josh is his son and he knows that. Yes, I do expect some financial help from him along the way."

"No more questions, Your Honor. I submit to the court that Miss Benson is attempting to extort money from my client Mr. Palmer by suggesting he misappropriated funds from his clients' accounts. As you can see, this is another one of her irresponsible acts. Therefore I believe Mr. Palmer should be given full custody of his child."

Lance looked at Faith smugly as if to say "I win. You blew any chance you had."

"Ladies and Gentlemen it is getting late. We will meet here again tomorrow morning at ten o'clock. Mr. Palmer, I am instructing you to bring the minor child Josh Benson to this court with you in the morning. I want to see for myself that you have him in your care. Perhaps you should also bring the so called video and any copies you have."

Faith was distraught. She looked at her dad, whispered the words, "I am so sorry you had to hear all of that," then fled the courtroom. The pain in his eyes was more than she could bear.

After the court room was empty, Lance's lawyer, Pete Brandin walked over to Martha. "Tough day, she seems like a nice kid. Would you care to go for a drink? There seems to be more to this than I have been told." They agreed to meet in half an hour.

Martha went looking for Faith. She found her sobbing in the ladies washroom. "You did a good job today." Martha said.

"Why did he have to do that, drag my name through the mud. He was just as much a part of this as I was. My dad had to sit there and listen to him tell those lies about me. How do I live with that? You tell me."

"Hang in girl. This is far from over, even though it may feel that way. Tomorrow I need you to be brave. Judge Harrison is a good man. He will be able to discern what is true and what isn't, then make the best decision for Josh. After all, that's what this whole thing is about. Now go see your dad, you need to be with each other."

SIXTEEN

The two lawyers found a quiet table at Tony's Lounge located a block away from the court house. This popular spot was used by lawyers who wanted to discuss their cases privately. Martha ordered a Pepsi, Pete ordered a beer.

"OK Martha, don't you think it's about time to tell me what is going on with this case. What don't I know?"

"Pete, this case isn't about custody, it's about control. Following an internal audit, over one hundred thousand dollars is missing from Lance's client's accounts. Your client is black mailing mine, using her son to keep her quiet. My client can bring him down; take away everything he has worked for. She wants her son; he isn't going to let her have him. If she does get custody, your client doesn't trust mine to keep her mouth shut. The baby is his insurance policy. If Faith is awarded custody he loses his leverage to protect himself from going to jail or getting disbarred."

"Will Faith do that?"

"She doesn't want to but will upon my advice, and if she is pushed too far. She has taken a lot from him. Personally, I feel that if she loses, she will end up going back to him and he will have complete control over her. That is if she survives her next beating and anything else he forces her to do. He is a sadist at heart."

She left shortly after that to return to her office leaving Pete to digest what she had told him.

Court reconvened the next morning. Today both of Faith's parents were there to support her. Faith could see that they were both upset.

Before they went into the courtroom, her dad took her aside and said to her. "Nobody is perfect. We think these things only happen to other people, we don't realize they can happen to us. You can't undo what you have done in the past, but you can move forward from here. I haven't been a perfect father, and I promise I will be here for you and your son from now on."

Faith was exhausted. She had been awake all night and it showed. Her eyes had black circles under them and her face bore the frightened look of a hunted animal.

When she saw Lance carry Josh up the stairs she started to run toward him. Martha put her hand on Faith's arm to stop her.

"Creating a scene won't do you any good. Leave him be."

When everyone was settled in the courtroom, Judge Harrison entered.

"I see you brought your son Mr. Palmer. I have asked Miss Williams of Social Services to entertain him until we are finished here today. I would appreciate the videos being turned over to the court. You do realize that you can be charged with making pornography, if the court so wishes."

"Ms. Simpson, I understand you have three more people you wish the court to hear from?"

"Yes your Honor."

"Go ahead."

"I would like to ask Elizabeth Heatley to come forward."

Lance gasped, then looked at his lawyer as if to say stop this.

After she was seated and sworn in, Martha proceeded to ask her a few simple questions.

"Elizabeth, if I may call you that, you hired Miss Benson. Is that right?"

"Yes."

"Why?"

"She was the highest qualified applicant at the time."

"Is it correct then to assume she did a good job for you?"

"Certainly, Faith did an excellent job. She was always on time, willingly put in long hours without complaining. Her work was of the highest standard."

"Would you hire her again?"

"Definitely."

"Yet, you almost fired her. Why didn't you?"

"I was torn. Her work was still of good quality but she was on a downward spiral. Faith is special. I thought that if I brought her into my office and scared her enough, I could force her to take a good look at herself and make the necessary changes."

"Did she?"

"Yes. I could see the effort she was putting in. When she became pregnant, she had a new lease on life. Although she was much quieter, her work remained excellent."

"Did Faith ever say anything to you about any missing money?"

"No."

"Were you aware that she investigated this on her own time and had the necessary proof?"

"No."

"Did you or your supervisors ever think she was working in tandem with Mr. Palmer and was covering up for him."

"No. We had no reason to suspect her of anything. When you gave the firm a copy of the files and her flash drive, we were completely shocked. Her work helped us determine who was behind the thefts."

"Who did your evidence point to?"

"Lance Palmer."

"Elizabeth, did you have an occasion on Devil's Island to speak with Miss Benson alone?'

"Yes."

"What did you two talk about?"

"She told me of the abuse she had suffered at Mr. Palmer's hands and that she was afraid being attacked again. I asked her if she could leave Josh with his dad in order to protect herself."

"What was her response?"

"She told me, in no uncertain terms, that she could never do anything like that."

"Yet, she did the very next day."

"Yes. Something serious must have happened that forced her into that decision."

"One more question. How was her relationship with Mr. Palmer?"

"She was very afraid of him. He was terrorizing her by saying he was going to put Josh up for adoption."

"Thank you Elizabeth. Your Honor, I would like to ask Mr. Amos of the law firm of Northrup and Amos to come forward."

"Ted, Mr. Amos, what was the result of having such a large amount of money disappear from your trust accounts?" asked Martha.

"Art and I personally replaced the money into the accounts. We wanted to keep everything as quiet as possible while we conducted an investigation."

"Am I to understand that you did this to protect the reputation of your firm? What else happened as a direct result of these missing funds?"

"We were forced into doing a major financial restructuring, closing one office and lying off some good people in our main office. For a while we didn't think we were going to survive."

"How did you?"

"Lance Palmer won a major law suit which put us on a more stable basis."

"Mr. Amos, were you at any time prepared to offer Lance Palmer a full partnership?"

"Not yet."

"Why not?"

"We felt that he hadn't yet matured sufficiently in his career to take on the extra responsibility plus we weren't in a financial position to expand. We hoped to offer him a partnership at a later date.

"Were you aware that Mr. Palmer was suspected of stealing the money?"

"No. Everybody was a suspect."

"When did you realize it might be him?"

"When you gave us Miss Benson's files and flash drive."

"Do you know Miss Benson personally?"

"Only to see her, Mrs. Heatley is in charge of our personnel decisions."

"Thank you Mr. Amos. Your Honor, I would like to call Big Ed Finley.

"Go ahead. After that we will recess until three o'clock this afternoon.

"Mr. Finley what is your occupation?"

"I'm a Private Investigator."

"Who hired you?"

"The law firm of Northrup and Amos."

"Why?"

"They asked me to investigate Mr. Palmer."

"What did you find?"

"In University he had been accused of a sexual assault but the charge was dropped. The victim left school shortly after that. He was also arrested twice for drug possession, but neither case went to court. He was barely passing, yet one of his professors that I spoke with, told me that if he ever got his act together, he would be a brilliant lawyer. He certainly had high hopes for him."

"What else did you find out?"

"Besides the fact that he prefers young girls, our Mr. Palmer has some very expensive bad habits. He drinks heavily and spends a lot of money on cocaine. Several times I witnessed him purchasing drugs from someone in the bar. He would often befriend young girls, some of whom may have been underage, buy them drinks and then leave with them. I guess he thought if they were in a bar they were legal."

"How do these young women get into the bar if they are underage?"

"Usually they have false identification cards. That particular place is well known for not verifying the age of its patrons. Several times I observed him pick up a young girl and buy her drinks until she could barely stand up. He always left with them hanging onto his arm for support.

"Is it true that you followed him out of the bar once?"

"Yes, once. He took a young woman to his car. By the time I got there, he was forcing her to have sex with him. Then he drove away, and left her sitting half naked and crying in the parking lot."

"What did you do?"

"The girl was in pretty rough shape so I took her to the hospital. I found out later she was only sixteen. Also as part of my investigation I checked his bank records and his income, I found he was spending twice as much money as he was making, yet he was not in debt."

"What does this suggest to you?"

"That he had another source of income."

"Thank you Mr. Finley. Your Honor, I have one more witness. She telephoned me last night asking to speak on Faith's behalf. I'm leaving this entirely up to your discretion."

"You may call your witness."

"I would ask Amelia Murphy to come and take the stand."

After she was sworn in Martha asked her. "You wanted to come and speak as a character witness for Miss Benson?"

"I did. Your judgeship, I am Josh Benson's nanny and Mr. Palmer's housekeeper. I have seen how both parents treat this little boy, and in my opinion, he would be better off with his mother."

"What makes you feel this way?"

"I see Mr. Palmer interact with the baby every day. He pays no attention to him and has very little patience. I got to know Miss Benson when we began meeting socially at the playground every week. She loves him. He adores her. It is plain to me that they should be with each other."

Lance jumped to his feet, "you're fired. Don't you ever come near me or my son again? I knew I shouldn't have trusted you right from the beginning." Looking at Elizabeth Heatley he declared, "you set me up."

"Mr. Palmer, sit down and be quiet" said Judge Harrison. "Thank you Mrs. Murphy, the court appreciates your comments."

"Mr. Brandin, do you have any questions for these witnesses?" Judge Harrison asked.

"No Your Honor."

"Good. We will meet back here at three. I will give you my decision then. Court is recessed."

After Judge Harrison left the room Lance turned to his lawyer. He was very angry. "Pete. What are you doing? Those guys are killing us. What were you thinking by not asking any questions?"

"Lance. I've known you since law school. I took your case believing that it was a simple custody issue. Right from the start you haven't been honest with me. I'm not going to put my reputation on the line to fight for something that can be construed as black mail. You should have told me about the beatings and the missing money. I can't properly defend you if I am kept in the dark."

"I am paying you. You have a duty to provide me a defense," Lance retorted.

"I have done my duty so far. I will see this case through to the end, but if you ever need a lawyer again, do us both a favor, don't call me."

Lance clenched his fist and drew it back is if he were ready to punch Pete Brandin in the nose. "You arrogant so and so, Just who do you think you are, treating me this way?"

"Hit me Lance and I will charge you with assault. Either way your goose is cooked." He walked away leaving Lance fuming.

While they were waiting Martha went back to her office to catch up on some paper work and Faith and her parents went for lunch. They didn't have much to say to each other. None of them were very hungry and ate little.

At two forty five everyone was back in the court room waiting for Judge Harrison. Faith's parents were at the back of the room chatting with Mrs. Heatley and Cassandra.

Faith sat at the table, staring straight ahead, desperately fighting the panic rising in her throat. She had been warned that the Post Traumatic Stress Disorder symptoms could strike at any time and she was using every coping skill she had been taught not to run away and disappear forever. All of the fight was gone out of her. If she lost today, she had no idea what she was going to do or how she could keep on going.

At precisely three o'clock Judge Harrison re-entered the court room.

"Miss Benson, do you have anything you wish to say before I render my decision?'

"Yes sir." Faith said standing up. "I never meant for any of this happen. My life here was new and exciting. Everybody was running in the fast lane and I was trying to keep up with them. I knew better, my parents taught me to know better. They brought me up with good morals and values, yet I chose to ignore everything I had been taught. I felt invincible, and never once dreamed that I would end up degrading myself to such a degree. I love my baby. I will be a good mother to him."

"Mr. Palmer?"

"Nothing more to add to what I have already told the court Sir."

"Ladies and gentlemen, after our session yesterday I listened to the taped conversation between Mr. Palmer and Miss Benson. I also reviewed the video you made Mr. Palmer. Then, after much consideration, I am awarding custody of the minor child Josh Benson to his mother Faith Benson. Mr. Palmer, I am instructing you to pay Miss Benson five hundred dollars per month from now until we there is a maintenance hearing.

Miss Benson, you have learned a hard lesson at the cost of your reputation and your dignity. I am giving you an opportunity to turn your life around. I am giving you a second chance. Use it wisely.

Mr. Palmer, you disgust me. The thought of you standing up here, defending the rights of others when you have such blatant disregard for the mother of your child is intolerable. No matter what the circumstances are, every person has the right to be treated with dignity and respect. I will be forwarding a copy of this transcript to the Judicial Committee with the recommendation that you be censured. I am also asking the police to launch a full investigation into the missing money. You are all free to go now. Court is adjourned."

As soon as Judge Harrison left the court room Lance walked up to Faith and began screaming in her face. "You stupid dumb assed broad, do you know what you have done to me? I'll get even with you if it's the last thing I do. You had better watch your back from now on. You enjoyed every minute as much as I did, and don't try to pretend you didn't. I guarantee that you haven't heard the last of me. I am going to appeal this to a higher court."

Although Faith was shocked by his outburst she felt exhilarated. Justice had prevailed. She had her son back.

Lanced stormed out of the court room. Detectives Don Sharp and Sandy Rowan were waiting for him.

"Lance Palmer, you are under arrest for the attempted murder of Faith Benson and for theft over five thousand dollars from the firm of Northrup and Amos."

Lance stood glaring at them. "Try and make those charges stick. I will be out so fast your head will be spinning." he sneered.

Mr. Amos, who had been standing quietly in the background, walked up to Lance and poking his finger into his chest said very calmly, "You are fired. As we speak, your office is being cleaned out and the lock changed on the door. I am also leaving strict orders that you are not to be allowed into the building."

A few minutes later, Faith, accompanied by her mother and father, came out of the court room. She was carrying Josh in her arms. All were smiling.

Before the police led Lance away in handcuffs Faith walked up to him and said sadly. "I loved you more than I have ever loved anyone. You were my world, my knight in shining armor. I would have done anything you wanted; all you had to do was say you loved me."

The next morning, she and Josh went to Lance's apartment. Mrs. Murphy packed Josh's things while she gathered up the last of her belongings. Lance was still in jail. He had been unable to find someone to bail him out.

She looked around the apartment and stood in front of the window. There were many memories here, some good, and many bad. Faith wanted to stay and hold on to the good ones for as long as she could. In spite of all that had happened, she didn't hate Lance. Maybe one day, when she was older, she would truly understand what this had all been about.

Her mom and dad waited downstairs for her. Once again the small car and trunk were packed to overflowing. She was going home for a while to get acquainted with Josh and make some definite plans for her future. Mrs. Heatley had offered her a job in accounting at a better salary. They would need her answer within six months. She was going to continue working with Mental Health until she felt she could cope on her own.

As they began their journey home Faith Looked at her son strapped into the car seat beside her and whispered softly, "I told you I would do whatever it took to get you back. I did, even though I had to lie in the process. I don't know who was driving the car that hit me. I never did see the driver's face clearly."

EPILOGUE

Today, on her thirtieth birthday Faith sat alone in her quiet office, wondering where the last ten years had gone. They had flown by so quickly. Her musing was prompted by a news report she had heard while driving to work this morning. The Community college was discontinuing the Legal Assistant program because of low registrations. This made her sad. If she hadn't taken that course, she wouldn't have met Lance Palmer. She wondered what her life would be like now if everything had been different. If she had not experienced all that she had, would she feel as satisfied and fulfilled as she did today?

Travelling back down memory lane she recalled the days after she moved home with Josh. The adjustment was hard for all of them. Josh was fussy. His little world had been turned upside down. He was used to Mrs. Murphy and her ways. He didn't know Faith or his grandparents, and Faith didn't know what to do with him.

For a long time she was nervous and suspicious of every sound, of every person who came to the front door. Her mom and dad rearranged her room so that Josh's crib was nearby. Many nights she had cried out in terror, always with the same bad dream. A car was rushing toward Josh and her feet wouldn't move so she could snatch him out of the way. Her screams would wake up Josh. In turn, his crying would wake up Faith's mother, and then her father would come to see what was going on.

Naturally they were all exhausted and short tempered. Amazingly Josh had been the first to settle down. What a little good natured sweet heart he turned out to be, easy going and undemanding. He entertained himself for hours with the simplest things. He called her mother "mama" and her father "papa". He tried to call her Faith but it was hard to understand.

Faith's dad became increasingly attached to Josh. On his days off from work he would take Josh everywhere he went. Other times the two of them would sit outside in the back yard, talking or playing with each other.

Faith and her dad were once again arguing every time they were in the same room. She knew he wanted to know more about what had happened between her and Lance, but she refused to tell him any more than he had heard in court, He was treating her like his little girl who still needed to be protected from the big bad world. She was feeling smothered.

One evening after a particularly bitter exchange she looked at her father and said "Dad please stop. I can't take this anymore. Every time you try and tell me what to do I feel threatened. I know that you love me and that you want what is best for me and Josh, but I can't live like this. You are doing the same thing Lance did. I need space. I need room and time to find myself again. Please stop trying to control my every thought and action. Every time I tried to stand up to Lance he would slap me around. What if we came to this point? I would die."

He looked at her and replied, "Oh my God Faith. I never meant to do that. I am so sorry. I guess I will always see you as my little girl."

"Dad, you have to accept the fact that I am all grown up and have a child of my own. I know this isn't easy for you, but please try?"

They hugged, promising to try and respect the dignity of the other. Faith also had to realize that the old grudges that she held against him were still very much a part of her life. She had a lot of work to do to forget them.

Their wound healed slowly. Sometimes she would catch him looking at her with the same wounded look she had seen in the court room.

She remembered how, a few days later, she had been awakened by a commotion in the back yard. Her dad and six of his buddies from work were unloading a truck load of lumber from the local hardware store. By supper time, an eighteen by twenty four foot cottage, complete with shingles and windows stood in the back yard.

She and her mom had served sandwiches and iced tea to them at lunch time. For supper they invited their wives and children for a barbecue. Her dad lit the fire pit, someone brought out a guitar and they partied until late into the night. The neighbors slowly drifted over, joining them. They sang, told jokes and sat around the fire attempting to solve the world's problems.

Every night, for the next three weeks, her dad would eat supper and then go out to the cottage. He wouldn't allow her or her mother to help, said he needed some time away from the women in his house.

One evening, around eight o'clock, he came into the kitchen where she and her mom were sitting. He picked up Josh and said to him. "Come little buddy, would you like to see your new home?" Then winking at Faith he added "you can come too if you want."

The cottage was beautiful. He had thought out and carefully planned out every little detail. There were two small bedrooms each with a double bed, a small closet and a dresser. The bathroom was located off the kitchen.

The small compact kitchen contained light oak cupboards, a counter top stove and a small refrigerator under the stove. There was even a dishwasher built into the side of the cupboard. A small oval smoked glass table with four matching black chairs defined the dining room area. The rest of the room was empty except for a gas fireplace at the other end with a T V hanging on the wall above it. The rooms were painted in warm earth tones with a dark hardwood floor.

She threw her arms around him and cried with joy. His unselfish act had given her back her freedom and independence.

Faith wiped a tear from her eye. She still missed him after four years. He died from cancer and she was eternally grateful that their last few years had been happy together.

The headaches had started shortly she and Josh had moved into the cottage. She could always tell when she the headaches were coming on. The pain would start behind her eyes then encircle her head like a vice. Everything was blurry, and often she was sick to her stomach. Her mom looked after Josh while she lay in her darkened bedroom, her hands over her eyes. If she had to get up the slightest touch, such as of the balls of her feet hitting the floor as she walked, increased the pain in her head.

She went to the doctor. He diagnosed them as migraine headaches and described a very strong pain medication. Faith only took them when she was desperate. She easily recalled the feelings of her first high and how wonderful she had felt. She didn't want take the chance on getting hooked on this medication too. Drug addiction would always be a threat in her life. Alcohol she could do without, but at times like this, the drugs tried to reinforce their hold upon her.

She thought back to the night her dad had rushed her to emergency in unbearable pain. She stayed in the hospital for several days until the pain was gone.

Finally she talked her doctor into doing an MRI. It showed that she had a healed skull fracture, evidence of her concussion, and damage to her neck. The combination of these injuries was putting pressure on the nerves and were the cause of her headaches.

Gradually the time between her attacks became longer. He gave her a medication to take as soon as she felt the first symptoms. Sometimes the pain in her head was not so bad, other times the headache didn't materialize.

At the end of six months she chose not to go back to the law firm of Northrup and Amos. There were too many painful memories that part of her life was over. There were still nights when she woke up craving the feel of Lance's touch upon her bare skin. The five hundred dollars a month mandated by Judge Harrison never materialized.

Gradually life settled down into a routine. She was still reluctant to go downtown. Many of her previous friends avoided her. Men were always hitting on her. That was the trouble with a small town; everybody thought they needed to know every one's business. After providing gossip fodder for a long time, she decided life would be easier if she stayed home.

She recalled the panic she felt the day the police officer came to the door and handed her a subpoena to testify against Lance. He was charged with her attempted murder and well as theft. Both charges were going to trial at the same time because she was the main witness for the prosecution. She also found out that he was still in jail; even his father had refused to bail him out.

Her mother kept Josh while she had gone to Lancaster. Her friends rallied around her. Cassandra picked her up at the bus depot and took her in, giving her a comfortable safe place to stay. Elizabeth picked her up each morning, took her to court, and brought her back each evening. Martha once again stepped in as her lawyer. She refused payment saying that she wanted to make sure that the scum bag got what he deserved.

Faith was on the witness stand for three days. Reliving her ordeal pushed her to the limit of her endurance. Lance's lawyer was brutal in his attack on her. He grilled her on the evidence of the stolen money she had collected.

"Were you his partner? Did you do this to get back at him? Did you falsify the documents to make him look guilty? Was this your way of retaliating after he beat you up?"

He went so far as to suggest that she had the beatings coming to her. His questions were relentless. The facts of the theft were plain and clear. Faith's initial investigation, Big Ed's evidence and the forensic investigation revealed that Lance was the person responsible for stealing the money.

Then the lawyer attacked her on the attempted murder charge. He twisted her statements all around, while maintaining that the concussion had left her confused. He went so far as to suggest she was lying. She couldn't have seen his car or his face. He had been nowhere near there when she was hit. His admission on tape wasn't accepted by the judge as evidence, because he said that Lance's rights had been violated.

He used her sexual encounters with Lance against her by implying that she was taking revenge on Lance because he had dumped her. He questioned her integrity and little by little he whittled away at her self-esteem. It was a terrible ordeal. Her picture and story had been splashed all over the newspapers and evening news.

Most of all she remembered how much Lance had aged while in jail. He had gained weight, his muscular chest and arms were flabby, and he had a pot belly which he didn't have before. His hair was completely gray; jowls had appeared under his chin.

Still the look in his blue eyes electrified her. She wanted to hold him in her arms, to make love to him, to once again feel the passion that consumed them. She blushed at her own thoughts. When she looked at him, he smiled that same silly grin he always used on her. She also realized that, in her own way, she would always be in love with him.

Due to her testimony Lance got ten years in jail for the attempted murder charge and five years on the theft charge and was disbarred. He would never again be part of her life or Josh's.

After the trial life had been good for the first few days she was home. After that was a rapid descent into her own personal hell. She thought back to the early morning she was pounding on her parent's door holding a very frightened Josh.

"Take him. Get him away from me. I 'm afraid I am going to hurt him. I stood there looking at him sleeping in his crib trying to decide if we would both be better off dead. He is coming to get me. I know he is. Lance will escape from jail, find and hurt us. I can't let him do that" she rambled on.

Her mother took Josh from her arms. Her father had driven her to the hospital. She was admitted directly into the Psychiatric ward where she stayed for the next three months.

After a month, the proper medication was found. She worked daily with a Psychologist who understood the complexities of Post-Traumatic Stress disorder. Slowly her sanity returned, and she felt that she was once again in the land of the living.

He convinced her that she had to accept the facts: yes she had made some messed up choices, yes she should have made different ones, but now she had to forgive herself for what had happened. These new choices could and would determine the rest of her life. She could use them for self-pity or she could use them to make the world a better safer place for others.

He helped her realize that Lance knew exactly what he was doing. From the first time she made love with him she was under his control. The drugs and booze were his way of breaking down her defenses making her dependent upon him. The beatings occurred when he felt threatened. The suggestion of selling her body to his friends was his ultimate power trip, but wouldn't have given him the satisfaction he wanted. She began to understand his fantasy was to convert her into his ultimate sex slave. Forcing her to have sex with the men of his choosing would have taken away her last vestige of power. If she hadn't given up drinking or gotten pregnant when she did, he would have continued to use her and abuse her until he threw her out onto the streets. He was a sick, control seeking man who never cared about her feelings. She was an object to him, something to be owned, nothing more, and nothing less. He even suggested that she had never stood a chance against him. Lance knew she was a naive young girl and used this to his advantage.

The psychologist helped her see that, in the end, she had made the right choices, she had chosen self-preservation, and through that she got her son back.

More than once he told her "many women wouldn't have been strong enough to make the choices you were been forced to."

Another thing Faith learned from her experience was that she had to help herself. Nobody could make her better or fight her battles for her. She was the only person capable of achieving this victory.

Shortly after her release from hospital, she enrolled in law School. She had discovered a new purpose for her life. She wanted to help others who were going through the same things that she had. Her parents looked after Josh. She worked hard, and with the help of bursaries, scholarships, student loans and hard work she compressed the five year program into three. She articled at the local lawyers office and was called up to the bar within two years. She never let up on herself, although there were times she could barely put one foot in front of the other.

Once finished school she openly championed women's causes. Instead of being ashamed of what had happened to her, she spoke publicly about what she had endured, and used this as a platform to address the issue of abuse toward women. She spoke to any group that would listen. She visited church groups, class rooms, and attended conferences. She needed to get her message out. In the evenings she taught a parents class on bullying.

Everywhere she spoke there was always one person who hung back until everyone was gone, and then quietly ask if she had a few minutes. She cried with these women as they shared their stories of abuse by their fathers, grandfather's, husbands, or boyfriends. All of the stories were the same, some more horrendous than others. She had the ability and contacts to get help for these people. There was one question that she could never answer. "Where can I go where I will be safe?"

With the help of the town and surrounding municipalities, she established a Rape Crisis Line. She tirelessly, and often without pay, championed women through the court system. She patterned herself after Martha always keeping in mind that she wanted the scum bag who did this. It seemed silly at the time but that was the driving force that kept her going when she felt too tired to go on.

She remembered the dream that she had been too afraid to share. She wanted to build a resource center to address the issues women had and provide a safe place for them to live.

It was a proud day when she turned the key on the resource center. Now women had access to legal, medical, and mental health professionals. There was a job center, a support group and, in an emergency, a spare bed or two. Someone was on call twenty four hours a day. The police, taxi companies, bar tenders and hospital staff all knew where to call if they saw or suspected that someone needed help. In the event of a rape there was always a woman available to begin counseling the victims before they left the hospital. They were especially vulnerable at this time and needed all of the help and support they could get. It was hard to get the message across; that it was not what they had said or what they had worn, and it didn't matter if they had other sexual partners. Rape was about control, somebody had forced them to have sexual relations against their will.

Throughout this time she had remained close friends with Cassandra and Elizabeth Heatley. At one point she shared her dream with them and they offered to help whatever way they could to bring her it to reality.

She remembered the day she opened the door of her office in the Resource center to find Elizabeth standing there.

"I've retired" she said. "I'm here to work with you."

She handed Faith a check for two hundred and fifty thousand dollars from Northrup and Amos. "Seed money" she called it. "This is their way of showing their appreciation."

After Lance's conviction the insurance company paid out. It turned out that Faiths' one hundred thousand was only the tip of the ice berg. The final amount that he had stolen was closer to five hundred thousand dollars. The check was their way of way of thanking her.

They had cleaned house too, firing the lawyers from the firm who contributed to her mistreatment, others for their drug use. Today they were considered one of the most honorable trustworthy firms in the whole country.

With this infusion of money Elizabeth and Faith searched until they found the perfect house for a shelter. Elizabeth worked tirelessly to get funding and the donations of supplies they needed. They gutted and renovated it and opened with room for twenty women and children. The proudest moment of her life was the day when she opened her House of Hope to their first clients. Of course nobody celebrated with her. She insisted the location of the house be kept secret to protect the women and children living there.

After her father died, her mom threw her heart and soul into working at the resource center, especially with the younger teens, who even at a young age, had lived with abuse. Faith's next project was another house just for them. She wanted a place where these young girls could continue to get their education and a find a place to thrive. She wanted them to be strong empowered young women. She wanted them to see themselves as survivors, not as victims.

She smiled when she thought of her plans next month – her wedding. She was getting married to one of the youth workers from their resource center. At first Faith had been reluctant to accept his advances. Still, in the smallest corner of her mind, she was convinced that she was damaged goods and that some people still saw her as being responsible for Lance's downfall.

Her fiancé, Allan Brown, was not like that. He knew her story. It didn't matter to him what she had done or who she had been with. Over time, he was able to wear down her defenses. Although she wanted to, Faith wouldn't make love with him until after their wedding. Her experience with Lance left her distrusting men. He didn't push her, and slowly, over time, she learned to trust him. Josh liked him too. He wanted them to hurry up and get married so he would have a dad like all the other boys. Elizabeth was going to be her Maid of Honor and a very pregnant happy Cassandra was coming to the wedding.

Allan knew her thoughts and feelings. He also had been badly hurt. The most important part was that he loved her, and in return she was not afraid of him.

They were going to continue living in the cottage for now and working as a team at the resource center. Together they were going to build the shelter for teens.

A knock on the door brought her out of her reverie.

"Come in," she said.

Her mother was standing there. "Faith, there is a young girl who has been beaten by her boyfriend who wants to talk with you. She needs our help."

"Bring her in."

A new day was starting, another day where she could make a difference in the life of other women. This was her calling; the job given to her from a higher power. Life was good!